Just Another Gorgeous Guy

Also by Irene Bennett Brown

Skitterbrain

Run From a Scarecrow

To Rainbow Valley

Willow Whip

Disobedience

Morning Glory Afternoon

Just Another Gorgeous Guy

Irene Bennett Brown

WISE WOLF
BOOKS

WISE WOLF BOOKS
An Imprint of Wolfpack Publishing
wisewolfbooks.com
701 S. Howard Avenue 106-324
Tampa, FL 33609

Cover design by Wise Wolf Books

Paperback ISBN 978-1-957548-45-6
eBook ISBN 978-1-957548-44-9

FOR

Rourke and Debbie and their gorgeous little ones.
With a special acknowledgment to my daughter, Shana,
without whose help this book would not have become
such an enjoyable reality.

Just Another Gorgeous Guy

Chapter One

Coming awake on a late May morning, Hillary Germaine thought again that a girl's seventeenth birthday isn't supposed to be one of the worst days of her life. How else could she classify last night, though?

Flopping onto her stomach in the big brass bed, she turned her face on the pillow and pushed a brown strand of hair away from her cheek. Her blue eyes filled with tears. Today would be even worse unless she could convince Mom and Dad that they had made a mistake.

Dad must be getting senile. Thinking that she'd want a plane ticket to Oregon for her birthday! Did Mom and Dad really feel it was all right for her to spend the summer helping a crippled old woman she hardly knew? In Reesville, Oregon, wherever that was?

Never mind that she had made her own plans for here in Abbott, Iowa, now that school was almost out. No, Mom and Dad were determined to send her off to *Oregon*. She'd bet that they still had wild animals in those forests. She'd rust from the constant rain. Or be attacked by some illiterate woodsman! Is that what her parents wanted? Oh, she was thinking crazy, but not by much. Rolling onto her back with a tearful laugh, she watched her coral comforter slide off the bed onto the plush, mushroom-colored carpet. Leave this? Her own beautiful room she'd gotten to decorate herself? No way.

She would talk Dad out of his dumb idea right away. Hillary slipped out of bed. She wiped away her tears and hurried to open the French doors that led out onto her small balcony. Maybe the morning air would clear her brain, she thought.

Shivering, she looked down on the terrace, then across the lawns, the tennis court, and swimming pool, to the peak-roofed Tudor house, the Dansons, next door. She would have to cancel this morning's tennis date with Colby Danson. She was doomed if she didn't have another talk with Dad, uptown at the store, as soon as possible. This Oregon scam was mostly his insane idea, she was positive. Talk him out of it, and Mom would go along.

Later, dressed in white shorts and a pink tee shirt, Hillary headed downstairs. It was no surprise that her mother wasn't in the kitchen. According to a note on the bulletin board, she was off to another of her aid meetings. Good old Mom, always aiding one bit of downtrodden humanity or another. But she'd left breakfast for her.

Lifting the plate from the microwave oven, Hillary took it and a tall glass of orange juice out to the glass-topped table on the terrace. Listlessly chewing her food, she relived the bad scene from last night. Not that her birthday didn't start out okay. Mom always went all out, especially for her birthday. The table was lavish but taste-ful, pure Mom. Talk in the beginning was warm, loving, happy. The food was fab, her favorites—London broil and rice pilaf. Then, just before the cake and candles, Dad undid everything. Beaming as if he were presenting her with keys to a Fiat, he gave her the airline ticket to Oregon.

SHE TURNED THE TICKET HOLDER OVER IN HER HAND with a laugh, not understanding. Taking her laugh to mean she was pleased, Dad's own glad expression expanded. Hillary looked at him curiously. From his neat gray hair to his trim mustache and dark, vested suit, Pop was turned out as impeccably as always. He was his own best advertisement for the men's clothing store he owned. But now his usual gentlemanly manner was gone, and he was behaving like a happy little kid. What gives? she wondered.

"You'll get to spend the whole summer in Oregon, sweetie," he explained. "And the Willamette Valley where you'll be staying is beautiful, just beautiful. Not to mention—"

"Wait!" she cut him off. "Wait a minute, please. You mean you expect me to—to—spend the summer where? In *Oregon?*" Her face screwed up in disbelief.

In the silence that followed, she saw her parents' smiles dim. "Please don't say 'Oregon' like it's some awful place." Mom chuckled softly. "Let your dad explain. Lawrence, do it right, honey. Don't go off on a tangent."

As if he hadn't already. He was burying her in his "tangent."

He leaned toward her across the table. "Hillary Gail,

up to now you've led a pretty marshmallow existence, you've got to admit. So your mother and I planned a fine, growing-up experience for you. How about that? My aunt Fay Renshaw has a quaint old inn, and you'll be staying with her. She's a widow, no other family. You remember the place, don't you, from our vacation in the Pacific Northwest? How old was Hilly, then?" he asked his wife.

"Ten. She was ten." Judith Germaine smiled.

"Look, guys, I don't want to hurt your feelings," Hillary began, as panic ruffled inside her. "Dad, I just barely remember Oregon, but I don't think I'd like it there. And I have my own plans for this summer. For right here in Abbott." She regretted the disappointment they showed. But they should have asked her before going ahead like this.

She could see by Dad's crestfallen expression that he believed she didn't know her own mind.

"What plans?" Mom questioned. "Why Hillary Gail, you surprise me. Last summer you complained that Abbott was dull and that you had nothing to do. You were bored. That's why we thought this was such a good idea. We thought you'd jump at this chance. Some time out West, on your own."

Hillary blushed. She played with her linen napkin, rolling it into a floppy tube and trying to look through it. A lot of kids would jump at this, she knew.

But this summer was different. Beginning in the dead of winter, she had dreamed about this coming summer. For a second, she considered telling Mom and Dad about it, then she knew she couldn't.

You couldn't say to your parents, of all people, "This summer I plan to spend every waking hour looking for Mr. Right, a guy really total. See, I intend to have this magical summer romance. An awesome romance I'll remember always. And I know where I want to look for this somebody special. The Serenella Playhouse. He will be a gorgeous actor from out of town. Mysterious, naturally. Only here for the summer. He'll fall deeply in love with me. Or—I might find my gorgeous guy at the country club. He'll be Robert Redford's son, someone like that, and—" No. You didn't tell your parents things like that and have them understand.

Solemn, straight-faced, she lay the napkin aside and told them, aloud, "I am dying to study acting. With the Serenella Players. That's what I planned. Or I thought I might get a job at the country club, for a new experience." *And meet him,* she added silently, holding her breath.

Dad couldn't know her true feelings, but he commented, "You've got the right idea, hon. But you don't want to stay around home. At some point, every young person needs to go out and learn to fend for herself, or himself. This is an opportunity for you to learn independence. Away from us, but still under the eye of somebody who cares about you. Family."

A thought came to her suddenly. "It sounds as if you're trying to get rid of me?"

They both looked startled, and her father reddened. "Nothing of the sort," he said quickly, but still as if he were covering up something. "Fay Renshaw is going to have hip replacement surgery this summer. She's had a hard time getting around these past few years. Now she's going to do something about it. When she told us in a letter, we called and offered to send you out there to give her a hand."

Like a slave? Hillary felt shocked and angry at the

same time. The fact was, she did enjoy helping people, the same as Mom did. Kids at school, giving advice when someone wanted it, or handing out a few extra dollars if somebody was low on cash. But she liked the assistance to be her own idea. This was different. "You might have asked me before you called her. Isn't how I feel about this important? You even went ahead and bought the plane ticket—!"

Judith Germaine shifted uneasily in her chair. "All right, Hilly, we apologize. Perhaps we should have asked your opinion before going ahead. Your father has been so excited about this. Neither of us guessed you'd be against it."

They were making her feel guilty, and that wasn't fair. She struggled against tears. Her father could be so opinionated, always sure he was right. And she couldn't escape the feeling there was more they weren't telling. She was struck with another thought, "Is it Colby Danson? Are you doing this to break us up? You don't have to. You don't have anything to worry about. He's like a brother. Cobe and I are just friends. That's all."

"Well," her mother began, "I have considered that it might be a good thing for you to spend the summer away from Colby. You two spend so much time together. I mean—all day long, almost every day!" she exclaimed, her chin outthrust. "As fond as you are of one another, and growing up…" Her mother's voice trailed off.

Another time, Hillary would have laughed. Feeling down about the plane ticket to Oregon, she couldn't even tease Mom. Instead, a sudden picture flashed into her mind. Of herself, waddling home from the Dansons' with her stomach bloomed out in front of her in pregnancy. The guilty father her sweet friend Cobe. Colby, with his swagger, his light blue eyes, and his wide, shiny forehead. She knew he was going to be bald, just like Mr. Danson. They'd probably have a bald baby, too...

"So it is partly Colby and me?" She shook her head. "You don't have to worry. Please let me stay home this summer?" Again, she saw the strangeness of her plea. Most kids would grab at a chance to get away from home —go anywhere—away from their parents' rule, and she couldn't blame them. But Mom and Dad were different. She got along with them okay, she liked it, right here.

"It's only partly about Colby," she heard Mom say. "Really, Hilly, your father's aunt Fay does need you. It will be good for her, too, to have someone from the family there at the inn while she's recuperating in the hospital. Actually, all you'll be responsible for is the little gift shop in the inn's lobby. I really think, once you get there, you'll find you like it."

Fat chance. Hillary sighed heavily.

"It's time you widened your horizons, honey," Pop threw in.

"Oregon is widening my horizons? You're kidding." She was tempted to remind them that this Aunt Fay person out in Oregon was technically not her relative. Except she couldn't be so mean as to remind Mom and Dad that she was their adopted, not biological, kid. She seldom thought about it, herself. It hadn't mattered for a long time. Mom and Dad seemed to have forgotten totally.

"To tell you the truth"—Dad stroked his mustache, then his chin, reflectively— "I wish I was going with you, Hilly. 'Rainsong Inn,' that's the name of the place. Doesn't just the name sound good, peaceful?"

"But-"

"The inn is nice," her mother agreed with a quick smile. "Very old. And you know how much you like things that are Victorian, Hillary. Won't you just think about it? You'd love it, I know."

Why did they push her? She was perfectly happy right where she was.

Dad got to his feet, pacing, waving his arms. "You're a little scared, chick. That's the trouble. Well, I understand how you feel. I remember when I was just a young sprout. Out of financial necessity I had to leave the comfort and safety of the family nest, go out, and get a job. Oh, I was scared all right. I'd never done a thing more independent than going two miles alone to the general store. But going off and making my own way right then was the best thing that ever happened to me. I learned to count on myself. I learned to make my own decisions."

Dad, not a lecture, please, Hillary pleaded inwardly.

But Mom threw in, "Your dad worked hard. Put himself through two years of business college, then worked up through retail sales all the way to owning his own large store. I don't know a soul who has worked harder."

Hillary fought against interrupting this ancient history lesson. Didn't they realize that they weren't allowing her to make her own decisions? Trying to send her off to Alcatraz-Oregon without asking her opinion was only one example. If they'd give her a chance, she could grow up right here.

She wished she knew what had really brought all this on. Why did they want to send her away? From the day she had come to live with them, when she was about four, Mom had loved having her around. Mom and Dad had always gone out of their way to be a part of anything she did. Fun with friends, her art, school activities, everything. The wholehearted interest they showed couldn't have been faked. So it was a puzzle as to why they were so anxious, now, to send her halfway across the continent for a whole summer.

Could they be disappointed in the way she was turning out? Was that what prompted this freaky plan? "Listen," she said through a tight throat, "why don't I get an apartment in town? That way we can visit now and then. We can have lunch together once in a while, Mom, and go shopping. What's wrong with my learning to manage on my own, right here in Abbott? How does that sound, guys?"

Her mother looked almost ready to chuck the whole thing. "Oh, Larry, I can't do this—" she began in a muted voice.

Naturally, her father wasn't crumbling at all. The look in his keen, usually thoughtful eyes, was determined. "She will go. It's only that the idea takes some getting used to. Hillary just needs time to think about this, then she'll come around. Isn't that right, honey?"

What could she say, or do? She had said *no,* she had tried to explain, and still they wouldn't see. So she'd think about it—think of a way to put an end to this dumb scheme of theirs. But not hurt them too much, either. She had to do something fast, or in six days they'd have her on that stupid plane. She tried to ignore the ticket that lay by her plate, while her parents made a vain attempt to salvage the rest of her birthday celebration.

With strained cheeriness, the three of them commented on the remainder of her presents as she opened them one by one. There was an emerald ring, her birthstone, that she had wanted desperately. Only now her excitement was more than half pretense. Her clothing gifts: olive slacks, a white shirt, and a yellow cashmere sweater, her mother must have chosen with the trip to Oregon in mind. Added to the plane ticket, it was as if she were being banished forcibly to outer nowhere. For no good reason.

Her throat hurting, trying to hold back tears burning behind her eyes, she managed to blow out the seventeen candles on her cake. But the cake itself would hardly go down when she tried to swallow. She hugged her parents, thanked them, and escaped to her room just in time.

She didn't want to seem selfish, spoiled. This morning she could honestly tell herself that she wasn't. She didn't want to go to Oregon, that was all.

HILLARY SCRAPED THE REST OF HER SCRAMBLED EGG into the disposal. There was another thing bothering her, she realized. She loved Mom and Dad more than anything in the world. *But,* she wanted the decision to be hers of how to spend the one and only seventeenth summer she'd ever have. It was only fair.

They would have to get their money back from the ticket. Exchange it for a trip to somewhere else or tear it up. That was up to them. But she couldn't, wouldn't go to Oregon to work for a person she hardly knew. It would be better for this Aunt Fay to hire someone in her own hometown to help her. Unless, of course, she was an old witch nobody could get along with. In that case, why should she be the sacrificial lamb because she was sort of related?

A while later, Hillary walked along the tree-shaded avenue toward town for her talk with her father. Walking would be better than driving the Peugot, she decided. She needed the time, needed to air her mind, and straighten out some things without the distraction of driving in traffic. Because, stirring inside her, was a feeling she had thought she was rid of for good. The old panic of not being wanted.

She had been contented for so long that memories of her life before coming to the Germaines had gotten fuzzy. About all she could remember about her real, biological parents was that they were often bent over books and papers at a table. From time to time they gave her some of the paper and a pencil or crayons, and she made pictures while they worked. Or she played with dolls on a lumpy couch. Her father sometimes drew pictures, too, wonderful drawings. At least to her small mind at the time. But was he an artist too?

She could hardly remember the rooms where they lived. But sometimes, she recalled, her mother and father took her to a park. The three of them played on the swings, or fed the ducks, and usually ended up having a picnic in the grass. She had been told that her parents were college students, very young.

They loved her. Vaguely, she could pull from the cottony memory of the past, a picture of their laughing mother and father faces. And she could remember their gentle touch and soft words as they put her to bed at night. They sang songs to her, often.

Then suddenly, the singing, the laughter, the hugs, were gone. A hated memory was the deafening, metal-grinding crash that took her parents away from her forever. Only she had survived the accident.

Three foster homes followed where she was taken care of, but not really cared about. Even a young child could feel such things and be hurt. She was miserably unhappy. Then, the miracle happened. The Germaines came along and legally adopted her.

Right from the start, she and the Germaines got along well together, although for a while she felt a bit lost in their magnificent house. She wanted so much to stay with them, to never be uprooted again. And she knocked herself out to please. Trying to sleep without disturbing her blankets. Fumbling to tie her own shoes and not need help. Going into a panic trying to hold her fork just right. Hillary smiled mistily to herself, wiping her eyes, as she remembered that child, the little girl she used to be.

Fortunately, Judith Germaine saw what she was trying to do and begged her to stop trying so hard, to just be a normal kid with a few flaws. From then on, it was love all the way, for all of them—Mom, Pop, and small Hillary.

Maybe she owed it to her parents to go to Oregon for the summer, if they felt it was that important. Still, she would like to get out of it if possible. Whatever—she'd talk to Dad this morning and settle it one way or another. And try to keep everybody happy if she could.

Chapter Two

Hillary entered Porter-Germaine's Men's Clothing Store, crossing the flagstone entry onto lush carpet. She looked for her father among the tidy racks and stacked mahogany counters. Coming here, she was often struck by the store's male elegance. It was Dad's habitat, and he fit it like a tiger in a jungle. But it was alien territory for her and Mom. Not that they were intruders here. Both of them knew a lot about the business, from discussions at home. It was just "Dad's place."

An older clerk winked at her, another nodded and smiled. Many of them had known her since she was small and had first started coming here with Judith to pick up Dad and take him to lunch.

Out of the blue, now, she wondered: What *if* Mom and Dad, one of them or both, were ill? Seriously? Would that be the *secret* they seemed to be keeping from her? If so, they would want her to learn to take care of herself before—before the worst. No, that was silly, impossible.

Dad was as healthy as a lion. Fanatic about staying in

shape. Always going to his athletic club for a workout. Mom was the same. She had regular physical exams; she took Jazzercise classes faithfully; and she was a nut about good nutrition. The nutrition bit partly because she had grown up on a farm and believed in keeping healthy. No. Dad got tired and grumpy at times. And he could be infuriatingly preoccupied and absentminded. But she would know if he was sick. Mom, too. That wasn't the reason they wanted her to leave. It had to be something else they weren't telling her.

Dad wasn't out on the floor so he must be in his office, Hillary decided. She hoped the old lion was alone in his cave. She headed for the back of the store toward his office, then hesitated behind a large potted palm tree when she caught the sound of her father's partner's voice, coming from there. *Darn.* Dad wasn't by himself. And William Porter sounded serious, almost argumentative about something. Bad timing. For sure she needed Dad's undivided attention.

She half-turned to leave when she heard William Porter growl, "I still think you should be upfront with the kid. Tell her the truth, now." She hesitated. Was she the kid they were talking about? She peeked through the palm fronds to see her father through the opened door, seated behind his enormous desk. His expression showed he was somewhat confused but that he was going to stick to his guns, anyway. That was Dad. Bill Porter sat in a leather chair, barely in sight.

"What does Judith think, Larry?" her father's partner was asking. "Doesn't she feel you should tell Hillary the whole story, what it is you want to do?"

Hillary stiffened. They were talking about her! And she was about to find out something Dad didn't want her to know at the moment. She attempted to move away, and couldn't. She wanted to leave, to be fair and not listen, yet she had to stay. Her heart pounded.

"At first Judy thought we were being selfish. Now she understands that I'm handling this in the best possible way. Hillary will be told the truth in September. If sending her to Oregon works. Right now she thinks she doesn't want to go. No telling how she'll feel once she gets there. But I owe this to myself, Will, and I owe it to Judith."

What did they owe to themselves but not to her? Hillary wondered. What was it they wanted to leave her out of? She held her breath, listening.

"It's true that the two of you have worked like dogs most of your lives," Will Porter concluded. "It's natural that you'd want to take it easy, enjoy the fruits of your labors."

She saw her father nod. "Judith has been trying to get me to take it easier for years. Now I've reached the point where I don't look forward to coming into the store every morning. I've lost my taste for it. I want to retire."

Only the surface meaning of her father's words were clear: Pop wanted to retire, to take it easy. Come to think of it, she'd heard him mention this quite a bit, lately. Not so earth-shattering. She turned her attention back to her father's voice. "...looking forward to selling you my half of Porter-Germaine's. Judy and I want to have some fun before we get too old. Is that too much to ask? Hillary's a young lady, almost grown up. She'll understand. I don't think she'll stand in our way..."

What all this had to do with her, his deeper meaning, hit her, then. They wanted her to be on her own now so the two of them could be together—*just them*. Enjoying

life without the responsibility of a teenage daughter,
whom they must consider old enough to stand on her
own feet without them. It *hurt*. For a few seconds she
could scarcely breathe. The whole inside of the store
seemed to tilt crazily.

They didn't want her! The realization was like a
blow. When she was little—cute and helpless—that was
different; they wanted her then. For years, she had carried
the deep fear that her adoptive parents might someday
change their minds. Not want her after all. But that had
stopped. They had shown her so much love, she managed
to bury the worry. Hillary-stumbled back a step.

"Your father is in, isn't he?" an elderly clerk suddenly
called from in back of Hillary, across the store.

She nodded, feeling drained in every limb. She
mumbled, "I changed my mind. He's busy with Will. I'll
come back later." She fled, moving blindly.

Outside the store, she felt as if she was enveloped in a
hot, suffocating cocoon. She should have seen this
coming. She should have guessed right away when Mom
and Dad wanted her to go to Oregon for the summer.
They'd tell her the truth in September? She knew it now!
They wanted to be rid of her. A good thing she had heard
Dad with her own ears, or she never would have believed
it.

He had said: *With Hillary on her own in Oregon, we
can prepare to take it easy, get ready to enjoy ourselves.
Retire. Sell the store.*

And yet, she would have sworn on a billion Bibles
they loved her too much for that. But they had given her
the plane ticket. Sure. They wanted to see if she could
manage to get along without them before they totally
dumped her. They planned her "going to Oregon" to be a

test. They cared enough to see if she was made of the right stuff, first. She had until September to prove one way or another if she could manage, alone. Big deal. Who cared? About anything, now. She'd go if that's what they wanted.

It was twenty-four hours later before she could say aloud to them that she had changed her mind. That she wanted to go to Oregon after all. To make it believable, she mentioned that most of the other kids were leaving town for the summer, and she might as well, too. She steeled herself against Mom and Dad's open show of relief and delight, bit her tongue against telling them that she knew the truth.

But she had promised herself to play their game their way. Wait until September for the actual word. Nothing she'd ever done was so hard, or hurt as much. During the remaining days in Iowa, her everyday life, her emotions, seemed shot with Novocaine. She was glad. Because she didn't want to feel what was happening, couldn't. She'd splinter apart. Somehow, she got through the last tests at school, the goodbyes, keeping the secret.

"Please don't, Mom," Hillary begged, when Judith revealed her plans for a last-minute farewell party with her friends. How could Mom be so insensitive? She and Dad were the ones who should be celebrating—their riddance of her. But she supposed they felt guilty and wanted to make it up to her.

"We don't have time, Mom," she protested. "And a lot of the kids are already gone. Cindi Mobley went to Europe with her grandmother. Lori Endicott is set to leave for Washington, DC, with her civics club. You must have heard that Jill Williams is gone. On a California vacation with her family, and she took Mia Reardon with her. Let's forget it."

"What about Colby? We can at least have him over, and his parents, for a small dinner party."

Mom was going to allow Danson the Dangerous Lecher to come over? Hillary thought to herself. But she gave in.

As she'd guessed he would, Colby nearly laughed himself sick when they were alone in the rec room and she told him where she was going. Of course he would think it was outrageously funny that she was going to be stuck in a place like Oregon for the summer. Like a brother would. And, like a brother, Colby was a pain.

Naturally she couldn't tell him the worst, that she was being dumped by her adoptive parents. That was something she couldn't talk about to anyone. It was hard to admit to herself, but she was working at it, trying to believe it.

In the last hours, Hillary decided that she felt almost as if she had taken on a social disease. It was ghastly to face—not being wanted. She felt in limbo, and numb.

The Novocaine feeling lasted through June third, luckily. That day, Mom and Dad—should she call them Judith and Lawrence now?—kissed her goodbye at the Des Moines airport. Then she was on the plane. In the air, hiding behind a book, she let the tears come.

HER TEARS DRIED ONLY TO START AGAIN, OVER AND over, as the hours passed, the plane droning closer and closer to Oregon. Was it something wrong with her that made her parents want to be rid of her? She had to face that possibility. Had she failed to show how much she loved them and did appreciate all they'd done for her? The beautiful home, the clothes, the endless lessons in everything she had had a whim to try. Lessons in art, tennis, horseback riding, swimming...?

Maybe, after trying hard to please them in the beginning, she had gone too far in the other direction. Grew lazy and careless. She seldom made her own bed or helped in the kitchen. But Mom had hired help who came by the week, and she seemed to love doing the rest, herself.

If that wasn't what she'd done wrong, what was it? Now that her parents were getting older, maybe they had minded her gang coming around? She couldn't deny she had noisy friends. They cranked the stereo as high as it would go and laughed and yelled a lot when they were having a good time. But why didn't Mom and Dad just say so, if that bothered them?

They'd seldom complained. Instead, they'd showered her with love and had allowed her to have her way in most things. Unless they felt she was about to commit something really gross. Didn't she show them enough love in return? She loved Mom and Pop Germaine as truly and deeply as she must have loved her natural parents when she was tiny. But maybe she should have *said* it more, shown it more, let them know how much they meant to her.

Hillary stared out the window at the clouds beyond the plane's wing, thinking if Mom and Pop didn't love her enough, what good would it have done? All at once she was feeling uncertain about who and what she was! Before Pop's bomb, she'd known. She felt secure then. She was got-it-all, got-it-all-together Hillary Gail

Germaine of Abbot, Iowa. Now she was back to square one. Nobody much.

She would have to get her act together somehow, this summer. She'd need to think about her future, and how to get there.

She slept for a while, then woke to hear the pilot announcing their arrival in Portland, Oregon. Aunt Fay would meet her here. She took out a small mirror and tried to repair the damage to her puffy eyes. She had probably set a record, crying her way across several states.

The airplane rumbled to a stop on the runway. Hillary got to her feet and moved stiffly with the flow of passengers from the plane and into the terminal.

It was a long time since she had felt this alone. A person could get lost in this mess, she thought. Never be heard of again.

She hesitated, wondering if she would recognize Fay Renshaw. She tried to recall her father's widowed aunt from that long-ago vacation here in the Northwest. Vaguely, she remembered a plump little woman. As active as a kid, although she must have been in her fifties or sixties even then. She would look different now. Seven years of arthritis had lamed her, Dad said, and no doubt she would be more wrinkled and gray. But in this sea of humanity, how could she ever locate her?

Hillary decided to stay where she was. She thought Mom had sent on a recent snapshot of her. Let this Aunt Fay person do the locating. Nervously bumping her knee with a flight bag she carried, she stood scanning the crowd churning around her.

A good-looking guy, well-dressed, walked by so close she caught a whiff of his cologne. He winked. She winked back without a thought, then was shocked. Being in this alien world had turned her weird. What if the guy tried to pick her up?

She was sizing her flight bag for a possible weapon—her bottle of Channel No. 22 would knock him dead—when she saw a silky blonde run to catch up with Mr. Gorgeous. He turned then, and Silky threw herself at him, gathering his debonair body into her arms.

So much for that.

Hillary looked away. Maybe, if she camped here at the airport, she would find a special guy for herself. Her plans for a grand summer romance could still develop. Maybe her guy would fly in from some exotic city, Paris or Naples, she decided dreamily. He would be as unhappy to be here in rustic old Oregon as she was. They would console each other, that would lead to romance—

"Hillary!" a raspy female voice interrupted her reverie. "Hillary, for Pete's sake, look over here. Here we are. Hillary!"

She looked and found a little old woman in a navy and white dress and leaning on a cane, several yards away. The woman waved. Hillary stared, then started forward. The woman didn't look familiar, nor what she expected. For one thing, her hair wasn't gray. She wore it in a curly black mop, aged Orphan Annie style. Perhaps it was dyed, would have to be if this was Aunt Fay. The tall, dapper-looking oldster with the woman was waving, too. For certain she didn't know him. She moved on, still feeling unsure.

Her voice shook as she asked, "A-are you Mrs. Renshaw? Fay Renshaw?"

"Would I be calling your name if I wasn't? I doubt it," the elderly woman stated as Hillary came close.

She felt stung, "I-I wasn't sure."

Mrs. Renshaw tapped her cane on the floor. "Well, you're here. And grown up from when I saw you last. Welcome to Oregon. You look citified, but we'll take that out of you in no time, won't we, Tandy?" She laughed devilishly up at her companion.

His grin was friendly. "Ed Tandy," he introduced himself, poking a withered paw at Hillary. For such an ancient, he looked good, well-dressed in a mauve shirt and gray trousers. Pop would approve of his taste.

"Hi." She managed a smile, although Mrs. Renshaw made her feel uncomfortable.

"How was the trip from Iowa?" the man asked. "It's a pleasure, meeting such a pretty young lady. Let me take your bag, darlin'."

"I can carry it. Thanks." It wasn't hard to imagine his reed-thin old frame tipping sideways from the weight of her bag.

Ed Tandy puffed up to protest with his hand still reaching, but her great-aunt Fay put a stop to any further argument. "The girl can carry that little old bag, Tandy. Don't think you can spoil her, put her up on a pedestal. Her folks have done enough of that, I'd guess. She's here to work."

Hillary began to suspect that Aunt Fay Renshaw wasn't altogether happy to have her here. Then her parents must have pushed her off on Mrs. Renshaw when the old lady didn't really want it! Humiliation warmed her face, and tears burned behind her eyes. She wasn't wanted at home; she wasn't wanted here. *What* was she supposed to do? She gulped to stop the tears. She couldn't cry. Not now. But she didn't like Fay Renshaw, and she couldn't help it. It was only a first impression, but the old woman was going to be grossly mean, she felt.

As though he had read her silent opinion and disagreed, the old man put an arm around her great-aunt's shoulders. "This little lady"—he brushed his lips across Aunt Fay's cheek and got a furious frown for his trouble —"acts tough. But she isn't. Your great-aunt Fay is the nicest, kindest soul in this country. And me, I'm just an old lover-boy, retired, who doesn't get to practice his manners and charm on such a young beauty as you often enough."

She relaxed, and her smile at Ed widened. He was kind of cute, for an ancient. With Aunt Fay, it wasn't going to be so easy, no matter what he said. Making an effort, though, she told her, "Mom and Dad sent you their love. They—they worry about you. They said to tell you good luck with your surgery, when you have it. They think it is a very good thing."

Aunt Fay shrugged, noncommittal. "What has to be, has to be." She dismissed the line of conversation with a look of impatience. "Standing on one foot and then the other never got anybody anywhere." She went on in a voice without warmth, "Let's go. We've got an hour's drive. There's plenty I have to do back at the inn, and these hips are killing me, just standing here. Tandy, get those baggage tickets out of the girl's hand. I think she's been struck dumb or something. Go get her luggage. Here"—she motioned to Hillary—"walk close by me so I don't fall. We'll head on out to the car."

Hillary tried not to show her hurt at the woman's rudeness. She took a short quivering breath and obediently placed a hand under Aunt Fay's elbow, walking slowly beside her.

What was she doing here, anyway? How could her parents do this to her? Her chin raised in anger. She was getting just a little bit tired of being manipulated by her parents and walked on by this—this *person*. They were in for trouble, all of them, if they thought this could go on. She had feelings, a mind of her own. And she wasn't going to be pushed around. She'd get out of this mess some way. And the rest of them could like it or take a flying leap!

After Ed Tandy departed for her luggage, she and Aunt Fay continued to inch their way through the terminal. Inwardly, Hillary still fumed as they waited outside on the sidewalk in bright sunlight. Ed returned, followed by a porter with her luggage heaped on a cart. She turned loose of Aunt Fay to make sure her case of art supplies hadn't been lost and tried to ignore Aunt Fay's remark that she had brought a lot more clothes than "any mortal could use."

A short time later, driving away from the airport in a maroon Buick, Ed at the wheel, Aunt Fay pointed to a snow-capped mountain in the distance. "There's Mount Hood." This time, her great-aunt spoke softly, in awe. "See that, Hillary? Isn't the mountain a beauty? It's worth coming all the way out here for a sight like that, isn't it?"

Hillary looked. The mountain was beautiful. She tried for a light, friendly tone. "We don't have anything like that in Iowa, I admit. Iowa is mostly flat. A few hills, maybe, but we don't have any mountains to compare with—with Mount Hood."

"Not telling me a thing." Aunt Fay was blunt. "I was born in Iowa, spent all my growing up years there. Before I started traveling around the country. I've held different jobs all over," she said over her shoulder.

"Receptionist at hospitals, offices, what have you. Clerked in stores, too. All that taught me how to get along well with people and got me where I am today."

Hillary almost choked. Aunt Fay got along well with people? Not by an eyelash! At least, not by behaving as she was with her. Or maybe Aunt Fay did get along with most people, but resented her. Resented her because she considered her a spoiled, useless city kid who'd been foisted off on her?

She chewed her lip, fighting tears. Spending months with this woman wasn't going to work at all. She looked out the car window through a film. She'd never survive Oregon. The next time the car stopped she should just jump out and start running. Or—she should hijack this Buick.

Chapter Three

As they were leaving the city behind, Hillary saw that they were ringed in by mountains on every side. Didn't Oregonians feel closed in, imprisoned? Or was that just a feeling she (condemned felon) had?

So many trees, too. Stands of evergreen trees filled in every area, it seemed, not claimed by a place of business or houses. She didn't like it, compared with Iowa's sunny, wide-open spaces. She wouldn't be surprised if all the people here, and not just Aunt Fay, were crude and uncivilized because of the raw, rugged country.

Even so, she realized that her natural artist's eye was taken by the awesome green of the landscape, the massed bright flowers she saw in so many places, as they drove along the highway.

All at once, Aunt Fay turned to look at Hillary and ask, "Do you remember anything about Reesville, where I live?"

She sat forward, glad for this show of interest with no malice in it. "I sort of remember it as being slow. A sleepy kind of place with few people. I-I remember a brown-striped dog named—" She thought for a moment. "Jughead! He would sleep in the middle of the main street. People just drove around him. Daddy said he was a town dog, he belonged to everybody."

"You can forget all that." Aunt Fay's tone sharpened again. "Reesville isn't like that anymore. I can't blame Charles Webb altogether, either. He's our mayor and a local businessman," she told Hillary. "Our downfall was that cussed city council vote."

"What do you mean? What's happened?" If Reesville had changed at all, it should be for the better.

Aunt Fay shook her glossy black mop of curls. "Don't ask me. I hate to talk about it. I never should have brought the subject up. Just thinking about what's happening at home sends my blood pressure sky high." She couldn't seem to forget, though, and she whirled to face Ed Tandy, beside her in the front seat. "You do still agree with me that the city council was wrong? That we should have stopped every bit of it somehow, before this?"

He nodded. "Damn blatherskites. But I'm afraid it's out of hand. When the ball starts rolling, that's it. Remember, Fay, there were just enough folks who said yes with open arms. That caused it."

If they'd just speak plain English and tell her what had happened. They were acting as if Reesville had been named a nuclear testing ground or something. Her parents must not have known, or they wouldn't have sent her here. Or would they? Honestly, this wasn't funny. "I wish you'd tell me—" she began cautiously.

"You'll see when we get there," Aunt Fay said in a

raw voice. "It will be a surprise. Or should I say a *shock!*"

Ed reached over and patted Mrs. Renshaw's shoulder. "Watch your blood pressure, lovey," he said gently. He intentionally changed the subject. "As soon as we get to the inn, I'm going to put out some more petunias. How about some big ruffled white ones, Fay? And some more sapphire blues. All right?" She snorted, but her narrow shoulders, bunched with irritability, relaxed a trifle. There was near-affection in the look she gave Ed. "You'll have us smothered in petunias, Tandy. But that's all right." Over her shoulder she told Hillary, "Ed is one of the best gardeners I've ever seen. He takes care of the grounds for me at the inn. My place never looked better."

"Why, thanks, sweetheart." Ed's brows arched comically at Fay.

"No need to thank me. I should thank you, doing all that hard work."

Hillary wished that they would skip gardening and let her in on what was happening in Reesville. After all, it was her life in the balance. But Ed was saying, "I don't do Fay's yardwork for nothing, miss. I live at the inn rent free, although I could pay. She won't let me. And I garden to stay in shape. Doc says gardening is just the right amount of exercise. And if I do say so myself," he added proudly, "I look good for my age. Miss Germaine —Hillary—how old would you guess I am?" Up front, he threw his shoulders back. He lifted his chin in a steadfast gaze down the road they had turned onto.

When she didn't answer right away, Ed turned to look at her, for too long. Afraid he would cause a wreck, send them into the ditch, Hillary said fast, "Sixty-five?"

He snorted with glee and jabbed an elbow at Fay.

"See? See there? You'd be lucky to grab onto this old coot, haul him off to the altar like I've been trying to get you to do." He glanced back at Hillary with true pride in his eyes. "I'm seventy-seven." He glanced at the road, then at her again, grinning. "But that's only by the calendar. Inside, I'll always be nineteen. Kid, maybe you should take a shot at me yourself?"

Hillary laughed. "Maybe." She wouldn't be surprised if elderly Mr. Tandy was the only eligible guy where they were going. If Aunt Fay decided to take him, she thought with a wry smile, where would that leave her?

She settled back against the seat, a forlorn feeling starting to creep over her once more. Aunt Fay and Ed talked to each other. She found little of interest in the bits of conversation that floated back. They discussed tourists, expressing the hope that lots of them would come to Oregon this summer and spend a great deal of money, but not stay. With the last remark, Aunt Fay gave Hillary a shallow smile.

The oldsters up front grew quiet then. The silence in the car stretched. Hillary continued to watch the landscape outside the car window, still feeling more like a prisoner than anything else.

It seemed like a lot longer than an hour until they drove through a further stretch of rolling farmland and finally came to a sign: REESVILLE. Her stomach did a turn. Ed said, "Prepare yourself, daughter. You won't see the sleepy village you remember."

What she did see made Hillary's breath catch. She slid forward on the seat, beginning to smile.

Ahead of them, the town looked like a movie rendition of a war zone. Huge, rackety digging machines tore into the earth. Rumbling trucks zigzagged about. Male voices shouted back and forth outside her car window, as Ed drove slowly through the town. *Guys* were everywhere. Shirtless guys in blue jeans and hardhats, young, *gorgeous* guys. Close, a bronze god about twenty, wearing a yellow hardhat, flagged them to proceed. More broad-shouldered young males steered the big orange digging machines, the trucks. She was sure there were a hundred guys, a blooming multitude!

Hillary couldn't hold back a fit of giggles. "What is it, Aunt Fay? What's going on?"

"Burton-Sipes, and they're not funny! *Burton-Sipes Electronics,* to be exact. The idiots had to go an' pick our town to build their new plant. Of course"—her tone grew nastier—"a plant that plans to hire twelve hundred people creates a need for more streets, more sewers, more housing. So they're tearing up the town, taking over, changing it, ruining Reesville."

This was ruin? This was Paradise!

"Like it or not, we got us a boom," Ed said dolefully. "Reesville is a boomtown."

She could think of a lot worse things. "I don't think I've seen so many guys near my age in one place before," she mused aloud. "All these guys can't be from around here."

"No, they aren't," Aunt Fay snapped. "They're college kids and others, come here from all over the Northwest to work for the summer in construction. Some have jobs building the plant, some work for the highway and street department. Some for Ma Bell, the telephone company. Reesville is crawling with them."

"For sure," Hillary agreed, her excitement growing.

Ed Tandy gave her a sideways grin, catching on to the fact that she saw the boom differently. "Most of the boys stay right here," he told her. "They've got a big camp in a park down by the river. The workers stay in tents down there, and some in campers and motorhomes. There aren't any of them at your Aunt Fay's inn. She had a full house registered before this mess began."

"If every room were empty, I still wouldn't give a one of them a bed," Aunt Fay said angrily. "They've got no business disturbing the peace, tearing up our town."

Ed looked worriedly at his companion. Again he steered the conversation to calmer ground. "Hillary, did you know your aunt's inn is a mighty popular place? You have to get reservations a year in advance, even those folks who come only for a few days, or a week or two. And Fay has live-ins like me whom you couldn't uproot no matter what, we're that happy there."

She smiled absentmindedly at Ed, her attention as they drove along more on the teeming activity outside her car window. They passed a small grocery store, then a restaurant, both doing a booming business with guys going in and guys coming out.

Suddenly, Aunt Fay leaned forward and waved at a lanky, dark-haired boy climbing from a yellow pickup truck parked at the curb in front of the bank. He was spattered with mud from his disheveled hair down to his faded jeans and rubber boots. A scruff, but kind of cute. His teeth showed white in his serious face when he spotted Aunt Fay. He waved back at her, grinning, staring.

Hillary's nose wrinkled. "What, I mean who, is that?"

"Nathan Webb, my good friends Virginia and Charles's boy," Aunt Fay said.

She remembered the name, Charles Webb. "Why

would the mayor's son be playing in mud, mud wrestling, or whatever he's been doing?"

"Nathan moves irrigation pipe, that's how he gets wet and muddy like that, miss!" Aunt Fay took offense. "He's a good boy. A hard worker. Most of the summer he's moving pipe or driving a tractor for Bemie Kelton, a local farmer. He probably was setting up pipe in the strawberry fields today, or in mint, getting ready for summer."

"They grow peppermint here," Ed informed Hillary, "and distill the oil from the plants to use in chewing gum, toothpaste, and stuff like that."

"Interesting," she said mildly, watching the mud boy disappear into the bank. With so many guys in town, she could be as picky as she pleased. Some of the out-of-towners might prove fabulous—college boys with brains, just using their brawn to earn some bucks. She might meet somebody with interests like her own, art, say, or books, dancing, tennis. She could hardly wait. This was going to be fun! She could almost hear her mother's voice: "Hillary Gail, you're headed for trouble."

Well it served them right, they'd sent her here. This was something she hadn't counted on, this boy-boom in Reesville. A near miracle. Why shouldn't she make the most of it, however she could?

A rock tune pounded and thrummed through the open window of a car cruising by. She recognized Rick Springfield's voice singing. Hillary turned from scoping the driver, a black-haired guy with a Tom Selleck profile, to catch sight of another dream, all tan muscles and sun-bleached hair, coming out of a place called the Taffy Shop, licking a stacked ice cream cone.

She almost drooled, and not because of the ice cream.

Without her being aware of it, Ed had stopped the car. She came to at Aunt Fay's harsh, "I said, 'This is my place, Rainsong Inn.' I asked, 'What do you think of it?'"

"I'm sorry," Hillary murmured, suppressing a giggle that she had guy-gazed herself temporarily out of the real world. She saw that they were parked in a paved area just off the main street. Looming over the maroon Buick's hood was an immense white colonial-style building, with endless black-trimmed windows and doors. "Nice," she said, "I remember this place now." Maybe it wasn't as big as Tara, but looking at it, she could almost hear the theme song from *Gone with the Wind*, *"Taa da, ta da..."*

Oh, Lord, she thought suddenly, *I don't want to go in there, I don't want to be here.*

Her nervous glance took in the wide front porch dotted with a half-dozen or so rocking chairs. The wide lawn was short-clipped, vivid green. Planted in a box of profusely blooming red flowers was a sign, RENSHAW'S RAINSONG INN. Yes, she did remember. She remembered a staid, creaky old place of many rooms that looked cheatingly new today, under a whitewash of fresh paint.

If she had any other place to go—but she didn't, at the moment, anyway. Swallowing against a dryness in her throat, Hillary climbed slowly from the back seat. She fell in close behind Ed and Aunt Fay as they started up the walk. Ed hovered close to the crippled woman all the way to the porch.

There, a large, elderly woman in a shapeless print dress leaped from a rocking chair to accost Aunt Fay. "Mrs. Renshaw, it's a good thing you're back. We had a problem at lunch. You better look into it."

"What now, Mrs. Coates?" Aunt Fay sighed, her expression one of long-suffering patience.

"Mavina made the hollandaise sauce for the asparagus too thick. I told her, but she won't pay any attention to me."

Fay Renshaw reared back so suddenly that Hillary almost bumped into her. "I don't wonder she paid no attention, Mrs. Coates." Her cane tapped warningly. "Mavina is a wonderful cook. Would you please not bother her?"

"But it tasted—"

"Consider that the trouble lies with your taste taste budsbuds, not with Mavina's cooking." With a lift of her chin that signaled an end to the discussion, Aunt Fay limped on through the open door that Ed held for her.

Hillary looked back over her shoulder before going inside. She wanted all that she'd seen today to still be there when she got a chance to check it out for herself.

She was slightly shocked at her great-aunt's bluntness in dealing with her boarder, Mrs. Coates. But the old woman seemed unconcerned as she fell in behind them. Like a curious, snooping weasel, she hovered, continuing to prattle about the sauce, about somebody named Abby who had been crying all morning, about the terrible stiffness in her side when she got up at dawn.

If the others staying here were this bad, it was going to be awful. How would she stand it? It looked like an old folks' home, and except for her and possibly a few others, it probably was. She didn't belong in this place. She couldn't make it a week, let alone the whole summer.

Her eyes began to burn, and she forced her unhappy thoughts aside, making herself look around at the interior of the inn here in the lobby. It was like walking into a past time. It *felt* old. But there was an appeal, too, a feeling that in this place life was simpler and more serene than on the outside.

Hardwood floors and bookcases filled with books gleamed from dedicated polishing. There were fat old sofas and velvet chairs in which she could curl up and read. The potted plants were real. She saw a registration desk, and from somewhere she could hear soft music. Not her kind of music, certainly not Rick Springfield, but pleasant. She must admit the place wasn't a total turn-off. On the left side of the back wall towered an enormous stone fireplace. And to the immediate right of that, a wide stairway led upward out of sight. To her room?

Ed Tandy excused himself to change his clothes and get back to his gardens. Mrs. Coates trotted after him a short distance, her mouth still as industrious as the dirt machines churning away outside. For a second or two, Aunt Fay stared hard after Ed and Mrs. Coates, then abruptly she spoke to Hillary. "Come on. I want to show you the gift shop where you'll be working. Today the shop is closed. Normally, we keep it open Tuesday through Friday, from one p.m. until five p.m. And all day on Saturday, ten to five. That's our best day for business. But you'll have plenty of free time. I just hope you'll stay out of trouble."

She wasn't going to get into trouble. But she did plan to make good use of her time, a la meeting gorgeous guys. To her left, Hillary now saw the gift shop, hardly more than a glassed-in cubbyhole. On one side of the store's entrance was a well-worn pew, no doubt for waiting husbands. A luscious fern trailed from a tall walnut stand on the other side of the door. Aunt Fay hobbled forward, grimacing with pain, and unlocked the door. Hillary followed her inside.

She saw that the shop's interior was done in cream walls with brown trim, Oriental carpet, and antique shelving loaded with gift items, glassware, books, brass figurines—endless stuff.

"I order from all over, nice things," Aunt Fay told her. "But I like to sell crafts for local people, too-like these wooden toy cars, boats, and trains. The decorative candles. Of course I don't take shoddy items. This is a business, and they have to be salable. But I do fine selling Oregon-made souvenirs."

Hillary fingered a small beaver made of pine cones that was glued to a chunk of wood carved to look like a miniature dam. It seemed a little corny to her, but maybe it wasn't to some people.

"You can't stand there daydreaming if I'm going to show you the rest of the inn," Aunt Fay said bluntly.

She made an offhand noise of apology and obediently followed her great-aunt from the shop. With artificial brightness, she said, "I can hardly wait!"

Immediately beyond the gift shop they toured a small room that was Fay's private office. Then she was allowed a fast peek into her great-aunt's living quarters, one room and a private bath. In spite of the memorabilia every-where, the room was tidy, peaceful.

She wished she could see her own room. But there was more that Aunt Fay wanted her to see first. They returned to the lobby.

To the right of the stairway going up to the second floor, wide doors opened into the main floor dining room. As they went in, Aunt Fay told Hillary, "This is the inn's largest room. I could accommodate any number of people, up to almost three hundred, although that would be crowdy. Folks come here for their anniversaries, wedding parties, or just to dine out where the best food is found. That's the ones who aren't so hoity-toity they think they have to go to Salem or Albany. My cook and head housekeeper, Mavina Immel, has kept bringing people back here for her good food for years. She's a fabulous cook, maybe the best in the Pacific Northwest. In spite of that remark you heard Mrs. Coates make. Don't pay Coates any mind. She talks just to hear her head rattle."

Hillary nodded. She liked this dining room, where the walls were decorated with hanging greenery and gilt-framed paintings of Old World, pastoral scenes. Back in Iowa, she'd had a solid belief that she would hate this place, but she didn't. Instead, she could feel a sort of lift as she looked around. For a long time now, she had felt an affinity for Victorian art and furnishings—everything Victorian.

The kitchen and food-storage rooms where they went next held little to interest her. The rooms were modernized, strictly utilitarian. She met Mavina Immel, a solidly built woman who gave her a brief smile before returning to beating a concoction in a large metal bowl. She was also introduced to Mavina's helper, an aproned, cherub-faced little man named Howard. One of the waitresses, Abby Ross, a nervous, featherweight blonde about twenty-seven, alternately gnawed on a knuckle and patted her frizzy hair as she was introduced. Although Abby's lips formed a smile, her hazel eyes looked sad and were red. Hillary pretended not to notice. It wasn't serious, probably.

Maybe she'd lost a hair in Mavina's soup and had been bawled out for it.

"I manage the inn myself," Aunt Fay broke into her thoughts. "But when I go into the hospital, you and Mavina will have to take my place. Ed will help, of course, he knows the ropes. Another time, I'll introduce you to the maids, Eleanor Bachner and her daughter, Patti, who come in by the day." Aunt Fay clumped her way down a long hall off the kitchen. Hillary managed a reply and followed. They came outside onto a wooden deck that stretched the length of the inn in back. Here were handsome wrought-iron chairs and tables and a few more comfortable lounges, chairs, and umbrella tables in bright yellow. Many pots of flowers added color and perfumed the air. It would be a neat place to get a tan.

Her gaze followed to where Aunt Fay pointed. Well-kept grounds stretched beyond the inn and included colorful rose gardens, an oval fish pond, a covered wooden swing, and three redwood picnic tables. Hokey, but nice. Ed Tandy, in faded coveralls, was on his knees planting sprigs of green in a patch of dark earth.

Directly below the deck, a gravel road circled from the parking lot at the front below them to a big vegetable garden far on the right, and then to a red barn. *Oh, yes, even a barn.* Aunt Fay broke into her thoughts. "I suppose a young city girl like you thinks you'll be bored to death here? You see my place as dull as dishwater with nothing to do?"

She shook her head slowly. "To be honest, I kind of like it, really."

"Well, whether you do or don't is up to you. What-ever the stuff you're made of will tell. My guests and me, we like it here at Rainsong Inn better than anywhere else on earth. We got a life that is down-to-earth and peaceful. That's important, with the rest of the world changing how it is."

Hillary could think of nothing to say to that. Aunt Fay continued, "Entertainment isn't fancy. But that doesn't mean there's nothing to do. We suggest walking tours to our guests, to see the old town that hasn't been torn up yet. We have some beautiful Victorian homes. Until recently, before I got so crippled up, I would hitch up my mare, Hannah, and give buggy rides around town. Yes, buggy rides!" she exclaimed to Hillary's look of amused disbelief. "And we've got the Homesteader's Museum. That's interesting to lots of people." Then she waved her cane, pointing.

Hillary looked. A shiny ribbon of river, which she hadn't seen until now, showed through a fringe of trees far down beyond the grounds.

"People can swim, fish, or go boating on the old Rainsong River down there. Or have a picnic on the bank," Aunt Fay went on, singing the praises of her place.

But it only made Hillary feel that she had come to a foreign country, or died. She closed her mind to Aunt Fay's voice and thought about her predicament, how she might still salvage her summer, her life. It wouldn't be easy. But there were, of course, all those guys.

Chapter Four

Abby Ross was elected to show Hillary her room. Aunt Fay couldn't climb the stairs, and the maids had gone for the day.

"All of the guest rooms are taken, yours was the last vacant one," Abby said in a wan voice when they reached the top landing. "The only sleeping rooms downstairs are Mrs. Renshaw's, on the south end by the gift shop. Maybe she showed you? And Mavina's on the far north corner off the dining room." She stopped at a door and turned a key in the lock.

Going in, Hillary thought with a sagging feeling, *No surprises here.* Oak furniture, quilt-covered bed, braided rug—she did like old things, but she didn't care to *Hue* in the Little House on the Prairie. What she wouldn't give this second for the luxury and convenience of her room back in Iowa. But no, she had to "pioneer" it!

"Mrs. Renshaw has a thing about mountains," Abby broke into her thoughts. "She says one of the main reasons she settled here in the Northwest is the beautiful mountains. She's hung a painting of a mountain peak in each room. All different. We sometimes call the room by the name of its mountain, like the Mount Jefferson room."

"G-great!" Hillary muttered, seeing that her painting, by the fine gold lettering on the walnut frame, was Mount St. Helens. What else? It suited. Her life was in upheaval just like the volcano. If and when things settled down, what was going to be left? Ashes? Rubble and ugliness, maybe, like the mountain now, as she'd seen on television. Or—nothing.

She felt like grabbing the white pitcher and bowl off the highboy and heaving them through the window, a little volcano act of her own. *Simmer down*, she warned herself. "Abby," she asked in a ragged voice, "do you like it here? Do you have to live at the inn, too? What do you think of Fay Renshaw? Do you get along okay with her?"

She was not prepared for the tears that sprang to Abby's eyes, and she instantly wished she hadn't opened her mouth.

Abby shook her head. "No, I don't live here. My two kids, my mother, and me have a little house on Whitman Street. It's not much, but it's all the rent I can afford." She sat on Hillary's bed. "I guess I like working here well enough. Your great-aunt is nice to me." She traced a crimson quilt square with her finger. When she looked up again, her eyes drowned in a well of tears. "You don't really want to hear about me..."

"Uh—yes, sure I do." Hillary nodded. What had she gotten herself into?

Abby blurted, "My husband, Miles, died in a mill accident six months ago. A log rolled on him. He'd just gone back to work after being laid off a long time. Everything—life, has just been kind of overwhelmin' since then. You know—trying to keep my job. Put food on the table. For the kids, my Keegan and Kirstie, and my mother who lives with me and looks after the kids. Ma isn't a good sitter, but she don't charge anything. I have to make sure we have a roof over our heads. To tell you the truth, I don't have the time or mind to know if I like—"

"Please, it's all right. You don't have to tell me all this." Hillary's face was hot with embarrassment. "I didn't mean to pry into your affairs."

"I don't mind. Sometimes I feel better when I talk about it. It hasn't been easy getting over Miles's death. I shouldn't say this maybe, but sometimes I feel so mad at him for getting himself killed. Leaving me alone in this predicament. Trying to manage all by myself." The woman broke into harsh sobs, "I just know I ain't handling things right—"

"Oh, don't, Abby, please." Horrified, Hillary hurried to the box on the highboy and came back with a handful of tissues. "Here, Abby, please don't cry. I'm sure you're doing just fine. With your children and everything." She kneeled in front of the woman and put a hand on her arm. "I think I know a little bit how you feel, though. My life seems a mess right now, too. Maybe we both ought to have more faith—that this is only passing trouble. Realize that we just need to stay on top of things. Do something to *make* our situation how we want."

She was coming on like a goody-goody, Hillary thought. But Abby Ross's problems were rotten. And being a thrown-away person wasn't so hot, either. She tried to gather her thoughts together as her throat began to ache. An hour ago she and Abby were strangers. Here they were getting morbid together. It was crazy, and funny. She stood up. If Abby'd leave, she might be able to get hold of herself.

Abby must have read her mind. She stood up suddenly, looking embarrassed. "Look, I'm sorry for dumping my troubles on you. You only just got here, after all. I'm really sorry. And you're right, I know. I need to think more positive, everybody tells me that. They keep saying my grief will heal if I give it time, but —" She sniffed. "I don't know. It's so hard." She scrubbed at her reddened eyes with tissues, patted her hair, and tucked her blouse more snugly into her waistband. "I got to go. I nearly forgot that I have to help get the tables ready for the dinner rush. Mavina is a stickler for details and schedules, whether with me, or the other waitresses. Last thing I need is to lose this job."

Nodding and smiling, Hillary purposefully steered Abby toward the door. "I wouldn't want to make you late. It was nice meeting you, Abby. Good luck. Remember to think positive." She held up crossed fingers. Abby grinned faintly and scampered out.

Hillary stared at the closed door a moment. "Whew!" she exclaimed then, throwing herself across the bed. Poor, sad lady! Anyone associating with Abby very much would soon be dragged down too, by all that gloom and doom. She couldn't stand it, herself.

She was close to falling asleep when a knock sounded on the door. She sat up, disoriented. Then she groaned and got to her feet, hoping Abby hadn't come back. But it was Abby. This time, she had a message. "Your parents are on the phone downstairs. They want to know if you got here all right. They'd like to speak to you. You can take the call on Mrs. Renshaw's office phone."

Mom and Dad, calling from home? "Oh, thanks, Abby, thanks!" She hurtled past the small woman, into the hall, raced down the stairs, across the lobby, and almost collided with an elderly couple on their way into dinner. When she told Mom and Dad how awful it was here, they would let her come home. Tomorrow, maybe. In fact, they'd probably already changed their minds about all this.

Inside Fay's empty office, she found the receiver lying waiting on the desk. She snatched it up and dropped into a chair. "M-Mom?" Her voice shook.

"Hillary?"

At the sound of the familiar voice, far too dear, something cracked inside her and tears scalded in her eyes. It was hard to speak. "Y-Yes, Mother, it's m-me."

"Are you all right, honey? You sound strange—"

"I'm fine really." No, she wasn't, but—

"How was the flight?"

"Okay. Too long, I guess." She swallowed to regain control of her voice. An urge to be mean, to get even, hit her. "Mom, this place is rampant with guys." Let Mom worry. "You should see some of them. I could go out ten times a day—"

"Did you have any trouble in the air terminals? Did you get lost ever?" Her mother was ignoring her remark about boys, or she hadn't understood.

"Of course I didn't get lost, Mom. I'm not a child." And she wasn't, although at the moment she felt like one. "Mom, can I talk to Daddy?" He would say he was wrong, she was sure. He would want her back.

"Hilly, sweetheart, everything okay?" His firm voice resounded over the miles. "How's Fay? You will help her all you can? What do you think of the place? You're going to like it there a lot, aren't you?"

So much for being missed and wanted back. The truth was, Pop wanted her right where she was. She fought not to cry, feeling as if she was strangling when she tried to answer. Finally, her voice took on a mind of its own, separate, and lied. "Yes, Dad, it isn't so bad here. I may get to like it. Yes, I'll help Aunt Fay." Lies, all lies. Why didn't she tell the truth? That it was the pits here, and she wanted to go home to Iowa!

"Good girl," her father's voice boomed. "We love you, sweets."

Now who was lying? she wondered.

"Goodbye for now, Hilly. We're glad things are shaping up for you out there. But I knew they would!"

"Sure, Daddy," she replied, feeling sick. "I love you, too, and Mom. Tell her goodbye, too." She shuddered, then mechanically she dried the tear-wet receiver with her palm and replaced it. She had cut the tie herself. Why? Now it was done, and it was up to her to stay afloat, alone, or go under. Dazed, a cramp of panic hurting in her midsection, she dropped back in the chair.

Dumb, dumb, dumb. She had had a chance to end this crazy charade, and she had backed down, flubbed it herself.

Because...? Deep down, she really didn't want to spoil her parents' plans for their together-just-us-at-last new life-style, she realized. And part of her wanted to take on the challenge of being on her own. Maybe see things through and find out for herself what was ahead, how it might affect her. Sure, having boys all over the place made the prospect more tantalizing. But that wasn't all of it. Maybe it was because she was aware others considered her a spoiled brat. Neither her parents nor Aunt Fay appeared to have a great amount of faith in her. She didn't like that. She wanted to prove them wrong. Anyway, it was worth a try.

Her pain eased away. Feeling good, in a way, triumphant, Hillary found her room again and tumbled onto her bed. This time it was Ed Tandy who roused her, knocking on her door, saying that it was time for dinner and she was late. Was it going to be like this from now on? She was so tired. She wished everybody would just leave her alone.

Ed told her, his spare frame filling her doorway, "The dining room is getting crowded and Mavina and Howard's grilled salmon and stuffed potatoes only go so far. Gotta step lively, honey."

Hillary patted back a yawn. "Oh, all right. Be down in a few minutes." She sagged against the door after he left. Then she went down the hall to the women's bathroom where she splashed water on her face in an effort to wake up.

Later, wearing fresh makeup, a lilac voile sundress, and cool, strappy sandals, she hurried into the dining room. In spite of numerous diners, and three waitresses slithering about, the atmosphere was relaxed, conversation a low hum to the background of tinkling crystal and soft laughter. But then, she thought, most of these people were antique humans, not members of the noisier generations. She found Aunt Fay, smiled at Ed Tandy, and took a chair at their table.

Aunt Fay told her, "I won't bother to introduce you to any more folks tonight. But I know just about everyone in this room personally. Most of them are good friends.

Local townspeople who like to take dinner here, and others who live here."

Abby brought their food. Hillary turned her attention to appeasing a hunger made worse by worry and uncertainty. Not that Mavina's cooking didn't live up to Aunt Fay's praise. She felt guilty, though, taking a third roll. She was behaving like a pig.

Her Olympic eating finally halted when Ed asked her how she liked Rainsong Inn so far. "It's old," she answered with a nod, wiping her mouth on a napkin. "I like old houses, almost anything Victorian. It's a nice place." She folded her hands in her lap and vowed to skip dessert even though Ed had said it was to be fresh strawberries with cream.

A flicker of pleasure had crossed her great-aunt's face when she said she liked Rainsong Inn. It was nice to make points without trying! Now, Mrs. Renshaw smiled at her. "You might like to hear Rainsong Inn's history, Hillary. It was built more than a hundred years ago. In those days, there wasn't a bridge over the Rainsong River, people crossed by ferry. The ferry operator and his family lived in a tent for two years before they built a cabin, according to local records. The founder of Reesville, Hugh Renshaw, an ancestor of my poor dead husband's, built the inn. Lodging was needed for travelers passing through here by wagon or on horseback."

"How long have you been here, Aunt Fay?" Hillary hoped it was a proper question to ask her.

"Long enough to come to love the place and never want to go anywhere else. That's how long. It doesn't matter in years. The inn was passed down to my husband, Stuart, and to me when he died."

Rising voices, laughing young male voices, sounded

suddenly from the direction of the lobby. Hillary peeked around Ed Tandy in his chair, and through the dining room door she could see Abby talking with two guys beside the registration desk.

Aunt Fay saw them, too. She shook her head. "Some young fools wanting a room where there isn't one to rent. They bother us to death, ever since this plant-building foolishness began. Who needs computers, calculators, and the like, anyway? Somebody ought to hang Burton and Sipes, whoever they are." She sighed, and grimacing with pain, struggled to get up.

"Aunt Fay," Hillary said quickly, "can I take care of this for you? I can tell them you don't have a vacant room."

Her great-aunt looked startled, then she settled back into her chair. "Yes, you can go for me. Just be tough with them. Abby doesn't seem to have any starch in her backbone. She allows these young smart alecks to walk all over her. Tell 'em flat out, no."

Feeling slightly giddy, Hillary realized that there was a chance she could do no better than Abby. But if she was going to meet any guys, there was no time like the present to get started. The two with Abby were both good-looking. The one in a white polo shirt and Levis was tall and red-haired. The other guy was a barefoot brunette, lean and tan, in forest green shorts.

"Can I help?" Hillary smiled as she approached them. "We're sorry, guys, but my Aunt Fay doesn't have a single available room."

Abby threw her a look of relief and flitted away mumbling, "Maybe you can convince them..."

The redhead whistled softly, then he grinned crookedly at Hillary. "Will you look at this? Stratton, son,

I think I've found the girl of my dreams." His blue eyes caught Hillary's own in an insolent gaze, teasing.

She saw that he had the dreamiest cleft chin—firm and very masculine, besides his cute, copper-penny hair. Redheads without freckles were rare; here was one. She couldn't have controlled her warm smile if she had wanted, which she didn't. The boy named Stratton seemed more serious than the other one. He lounged against the registration desk. "Don't you even have a closet we can sleep in? We're sick of our tent. It's supposed to rain tonight. Ever sleep in a leaky tent?"

"I really am sorry," she told them. "I understand that the town is packed. I know I'd hate a tent. I guess I'm lucky that my Aunt Fay saved me a room. I don't know what else to tell you—"

"I know what you can tell me," the redhead said, pulling a fistful of his shirtfront away from his chest and thumping it in and out as though his heart was beating hard. "Tell me you're my girl from this minute on."

Stratton, giving up talk of the room, joined in to tease, "Take me, sweetheart. Cary is a jerk. He's got nothing going for him but money. I'm the one with the personality and good looks."

"Whoa," Cary protested. "A guy whose hero is Garfield the cat has to be okay, and that's me, Blake the Great."

"Shhh." Hillary giggled. "I'm supposed to be getting rid of you guys." She motioned. "There's the door. My great-aunt carries a cane; we don't want her coming out here after you. She has a low opinion of people connected with this Burton-Sipes project. You work for them?"

"And proud of it." The copper-penny guy shoved out

his delicious chin. "You're looking at Cary Blake, head hammer-pounder. My buddy here is Stratton Smith, chief nail-sorter. We keep Burton-Sipes going. Now, it's your turn. How'd you happen to land in a place like this, the way you look?"

They followed as she led toward the door. "I'm an orphan," she said with a pout over her shoulder, only half-kidding. "Cast aside by uncaring parents. The truth is, I've been sentenced for the summer to Reesville to help out here at the inn while my dad's aunt has surgery. She's Mrs. Renshaw, owner of this place. I'd rather be at home in Iowa, but that's another story. My name is Hillary Germaine."

"Wait." The one named Cary Blake held up his hand to halt them. His eyes took in each individual feature of her face so slowly she blushed. "I don't suppose a nice Iowa girl named Hillary Germaine would want to share *her* room? With two homeless, but strictly safe and gentlemanly guys?"

"Who don't want to drown like rats?" Stratton Smith appealed.

"Oh, you guys, please get out of here, you're crazy." She laughed. "If my great-aunt doesn't have a rule about co-habitation now, I'm sure she'd make one in the blink of an eye. I doubt if you'd like it here, anyway. Almost all of the residents were born in the last century, I think. It isn't a muddy tent, but something tells me that living here will be like living in a museum."

"You know, Stratt," Cary Blake announced with a grin. "I think this girl needs cheering up. We're going to have to come around here to see her, often."

"It's our duty," Stratton agreed. "How about a Coke, right now? I'll buy the first round."

"Whew!" Cary exclaimed, genuine surprise on his face. "The love bug did bite you if you're willing to release a whole buck and a half. Heeyyy, Stratton! This guy," he told Hillary, "can squeeze a coin until it cries."

"Cut it out, Cary." Stratton looked embarrassed, half angry. "Not everybody has gold-plated parents like you do. Some of us aren't here on the project just for kicks, because our friends are here. Some of us have to work for the dough to stay in college—"

"Look," Hillary pleaded, "don't argue. I can't go with you, anyway. This is my first night here. I'm really beat. But some other time. Honest, I'd like to get to know you both better."

"All right," Cary said, "but if any other jokers from this project discover you're here, cut 'em off at the pass. Me and Stratt are first in line for your gorgeous company. Don't forget. Let's go, airhead," he genially ordered his friend.

Hillary held the door open. "I don't think there is a way I could forget either of you!" She laughed. "Bye, guys."

"Back to the muddy trenches," she heard Stratton moan as they headed down the sidewalk. "Dad didn't tell me leaving home would be like this. Work is hell."

In the future, she decided, she really should go out with them, ease their misery with her choice feminine company. Although, at the moment, neither of them appealed as Mr. Right—exactly.

Chapter Five

"From your expression, Hillary," Aunt Fay said when she returned to the dining room, "you enjoyed clearing up matters out there in the lobby. You were gone long enough."

"A couple of boys are tired of living in a tent. They understood about your rooms being filled. Abby had it under control. Nice guys, they just wanted to talk." She sat down again at the table.

"Humph," Aunt Fay grunted, scrutinizing her, "I suppose you'll want companionship with other young people. Otherwise you'll get lonesome and want to run back to Iowa. But be careful. I wouldn't trust some of these upstarts from out of town any further than I could throw them. Never know what they're into—drugs, drink, who knows? Charles Webb, Nathan's dad, once had a nice lounge. This new crowd in town is fast turning his bar into a dump, a hell-hole. But, as mayor of this town, he ought to've done more to keep Burton-Sipes out. Instead of trying to please that small majority. Now he's paying. We all are."

"I'll be careful, Aunt Fay. You needn't worry." She shook her head. "Those boys, Cary and Stratton, a few minutes ago asked me to go with them tonight. I said no. I intend to take my time and not go out with anyone I don't feel sure about."

Aunt Fay's eyebrows rose. "You surprise me," she said. "I didn't expect you to be sensible. How about that? I figured Judith and Lawrence would have petted and pampered you so much you wouldn't be worth shoot."

"No," Hillary answered tartly, "I'm not a total mess. You have to give Mom and Dad a little credit." Even if they no longer wanted her around. She picked up her glass of milk, but a painful lump forming in her throat forced her to put it down again.

Wanting to change the subject, she looked at Ed Tandy, to talk. But he was on a trip with his strawberries. She had to get out of here. She was about to ask to be excused when Abby Ross appeared to clear the table. As the young woman gathered up the dishes, the cups danced dangerously in their saucers. Hillary caught Aunt Fay's look of muffled exasperation, but her great-aunt didn't say anything. She was relieved, knowing that a scolding would only make Abby's nerves worse. Poor soul, maybe she'd snap out of it soon. It would truly be the pits if Abby lost her job on top of everything else.

～

NEXT MORNING, HILLARY WOKE TO THE SOUND OF drizzling rain. What else could she expect, her first morning in rainy Oregon? Disgruntled, she went to breakfast. "Can you entertain yourself today?" Aunt Fay asked after they'd finished. "I have a lot of paperwork to do in my office, things I have to take care of before I check into the hospital in a few weeks."

"Sure, go ahead." Hillary sighed moodily. "I wanted to see the town this morning anyway. But I think I'll wait until it quits raining."

As her great-aunt crept to her feet, she hooted with laughter. "In that case, you may be sitting here until doomsday. Real Oregonians don't let a little shower keep them from anything. They splash around like ducks, they love it."

She raised her glass in a mock cheer. *But I'm not an Oregonian*, she thought silently.

By late afternoon the showers ceased, the sun came out, warm, drying. Feeling as though she'd been jailed all day, Hillary left the inn in a hurry, to roam.

Arriving yesterday afternoon, the young male population swarming the town had been foremost in her mind. (And wasn't far from her thoughts today.) But now she also saw what Aunt Fay made such a fuss about: the disrupted landscape itself. Street-corner ditches were fenced off with Do Not Trespass signs. Boards were down where cement sidewalks had been riddled. Piles of rock and sand were all over. From more than one direction, she could hear the nasty grind and growl of bulldozers gashing away.

Going north, she came to the Homesteaders' Museum Aunt Fay mentioned. The tiny old building was set back from the street, across from where she stood. A huge crane towered over it like a giant insect on one side. Close on the other side, a man was climbing down from a caterpillar tractor. There was something unfair in the sight, as if the museum didn't have a chance, was being unfairly overpowered. She could see Aunt Fay's point. It was like—*wrong.*

Noting the young driver in a passing yellow highway department truck, she thought, *But how could anything bringing this many guys to one place be all bad?* And seriously, didn't the hillbillies here know the advantages that would follow with the plant? They'd probably get a new library, a theater, all kinds of goodies. But never having had them, they didn't realize what they were missing.

She went on, discovering an interesting-looking antique shop and a few other stores. At the Taffy Shop, she went in, thinking to have a quick Coke and possibly see Cary Blake and Stratton Smith.

The small café was crowded and noisy. She bought a large praline ice cream cone and made her way to the door again. She hadn't seen any sign of the only boys she had met. A voice called as she went through the door, "Hey, baby, come back again." She smiled to herself. Oh, she'd be back. For sure. This summer she'd need places to get away to, away from the inn.

Turning in the opposite direction, she walked several blocks south. The din of construction was louder this way. Finally, she came to Reesville's bone of contention, the main plant project. "BURTON-SIPES ELECTRONICS PLANT, Under Construction," a huge sign proclaimed.

It was too much. The plant was out of sync with the rest of Reesville. Under the hands of workers, the metal skeleton of a monstrous building was being fleshed with concrete and wood. This centered several acres, which eventually, she supposed, would be paved, planted to grounds, or maybe it was space for more buildings.

The ultra-modern building was an eyesore, compared with the quaint houses and yards that made up the rest of the town. Why didn't they leave this place alone, why did it have to change? It startled Hillary, to have such an opinion. Amazing that she would actually agree with Aunt Fay. But the plant should have been located elsewhere. In a town more progressive, more interested in money and growth. It was sad, for gosh sakes.

She should make up her mind, though. A place couldn't have it both ways, or could it? With a sigh of agitation, she turned toward the inn. Either way, standing still or going ahead, this town had nothing to do with her. She might be stuck here in Reesville for the summer, but it wasn't a life sentence. After this summer she would be —somewhere else. And the people who lived here would have to deal with *whatever*. They might like some of the better changes. But she—

A sudden noise behind her made Hillary jump, losing her thoughts. She saw that it was a basketball that had smacked the sidewalk and now it rolled to a stop at the curb. If some guy wanted her attention, why didn't he just whistle? She whirled. A tall blonde girl smiled at her apologetically. "Didn't mean to use you for a bowling pin, almost," she told Hillary, rubbing her hands down the sides of her baby blue shorts. Her matching tee shirt said SAN FRANCISCO across the front. "I think I'm losing my touch. Can't even hang onto the ball anymore." She caught the ball as Hillary tossed it back.

"It's okay." She smiled. "But for a minute I did think I was being ambushed. I'm new here. Hillary Germaine is my name."

The blonde dribbled the basketball on the sidewalk in a near dance, her short hair flipping in the air. "Leilani

Haffner," she panted, "but call me Lei, please. I hate my name." She caught the ball and held it against her chest. "Is your old man here for a construction job? Mine can probably help him if he doesn't have one lined up."

Hillary couldn't help laughing. "No, my father has his own—*work*, back in Iowa. I'm here by myself. I came out this summer to help my great-aunt in the giftshop over at Rainsong Inn."

Lei shook her feathered blonde bangs back from her forehead, looking at her. "Oh, that place, Rainsong Inn. Mom and Dad and I spent a few nights in that stodgy old castle before we found our house to rent, over on Albee Street."

"I only just got here," Hillary protested, "but the place doesn't seem that bad." Funny that she was defending it, as much as she didn't want to be here!

"Oh, I don't have anything against the inn. I didn't mean that. Wrong choice of words, I guess. The thing is, we move around a lot because of Dad's work. Mom and I just hate any kind of motel or hotel because we've stayed in so many of them. We like a regular house, you know? Dad took this job as foreman for one of the construction crews at the plant, but Mom hopes it's his last job. She wants him to retire. In fact, if we stayed here for good, it would be all right with the two of us."

Everyone to their own tastes, Hillary thought. Aloud, she said, "I'm glad to know there is someone in town to talk to. Stop in at the Rainsong gift shop sometime, even if you don't like the rest of the place."

"Hey, I will." Leilani started to dribble the ball again. "Do you play?" She caught the ball and held it toward Hillary.

"Not at all, sorry. My P. E. coach back in Abbott,

Iowa, used to bug me to try, because I'm tall. But I never seemed to be any good at it. You handle the ball like a pro, though, Lei."

"Let me tell you, I'm the almost star of so many basketball teams, I've lost count. I never attended one school long enough to make it clear to the top. But I'm going to play college ball if I can get good enough."

A few years from now, more than for her, Hillary decided. Leilani looked around fifteen, maybe close to sixteen. She told Lei, "I'll bet you make it big. That ball looks like magic in your hands."

"Thanks. So what's your thing, Hillary? Is running the gift shop special with you? Do you want to do something like that, permanent?"

"Please! You've got to be kidding! I haven't thought much about it—well, some." She was silent a moment, realizing that she hadn't thought much about her future— it always seemed so far away. Now, though, she'd better think about it. Like Lei's basketball, her life had been placed in her hands; it was her game now. "It might be great to study art," she said slowly, "in a place like, you know, Paris. Don't laugh. Maybe I'll marry a rich guy, a prince or something. Travel the world." By now, she was laughing, too. "Of course, all that can happen only if I don't die young, first, of boredom here in Reesville."

"I suppose there is a danger of that." Leilani giggled. "But have you checked out the guys in this place?"

She called, dribbling the ball in a lithe, tricky step on down the sidewalk, "I'm late getting home. I was supposed to help Mom with some housework this afternoon. I'll see you again, okay?"

"Sure. Bye." Leilani might be a little younger, but she appeared to be a neat girl. The boys, Cary Blake and

Stratton Smith, were good guys. It was looking more and more like her summer wouldn't be a total holocaust.

Going home, she looked up to see Abby Ross, evidently off duty, coming toward her along a section of broken sidewalk. With Abby were two small, blond children—a boy and a girl—and a frowzy-looking older woman, probably her mother. Hillary turned quickly back in the opposite direction, hoping she hadn't been seen. No way could she take Abby's gloom and doom right now. Yesterday's dose was enough. Furtively, she glanced back over her shoulder and saw the small family shuffle into a supermarket. With a sigh, feeling a trifle guilty, she turned about and hurried toward the inn.

THE DRIZZLE CONTINUED THE NEXT FEW DAYS. HILLARY looked out the shop window, the end of that first week, to see the mayor's son, Nathan Webb, helping Ed. Aunt Fay talked about Nathan a lot, she was impressed with him. This afternoon, he and Ed were loading limbs trimmed from shrubs and other yard debris into the back of Nathan's yellow pickup truck. Why not get to know the guy if he was going to be around? She decided, with a little lurch of excitement.

She waited until there was a lull in the shop, and in the rain, then she slipped outside to watch them, ducking under the inn roof overhang in case it showered again. She hugged herself with her arms, watching the old man and Nathan deep in conversation as they worked, unaware of her. After another moment, she called, "Hi, Ed!"

The guy, Nathan, whirled as though he'd been shot at.

Then, he covered up with a calm, nonchalant grin before turning a square-shouldered back to her.

Sure.

"There's my girlfriend," Ed Tandy told him, grabbing Nathan's arm, turning him back around. "Nathan, I want you to meet Hillary Germaine. Isn't the girl an eyeful? She's here for the summer from Iowa—"

"I know about her." Nathan had the nicest smile. In fact, he was a whole lot better looking, cleaned up from his irrigation togs, than she would have guessed. Her heart skipped a beat, looking him over. With so many guys like this around, how could a girl ever choose?

He stared at her, although he seemed unaware of it. Then, a stickery branch he was tossing into the pickup snagged his finger. "Ouch!" He shook his hand, and his face turned crimson.

Hillary smothered a giggle, but not before he saw that she thought it was funny. They grinned at one another.

"Nathan didn't have to irrigate 'cause of the rain." Ed jarred their attention from one another back to him. "So he came to help me. I missed his dad's Wednesday night council meeting so he's been filling me in. When the zoning argument came up, what then?" he asked Nathan, leaning against the truck, his face screwed up with curious concern.

Darn. They were going back to their earlier conversation. Hillary felt deflated, but she waited, listening, hoping they wouldn't leave her out.

Nathan talked while he worked, speaking earnestly of "revenue bonds, zoning, single-dwelling housing" and a whole lot more alien to her ears. So alien, she was afraid she would go to sleep on her feet, in spite of the chill in the air. It all had to do with the Burton-Sipes Electronics

Plant. Didn't the people in this hick town know anything else? Poor Nathan, with his dad the mayor, he must have to listen to boring small town politics all the time. How could he stand it? It was like her having to hear Dad talk about men's suits and socks and how to sell them, back home.

But she had to admit, Nathan was acting interested in what he was telling Ed. Too bad that civics, political science, and any such thing were her worst subjects. She listened, hoping to make sense of what Ed and Nathan were talking about as they scrambled back and forth, picking up brush. But their words were so much mumbo-jumbo to her. Anyway, they had plainly forgotten her. She headed back inside. Neither Ed nor Nathan paid attention to her leaving. In the shop, she realized angrily that she had gotten her shoes muddy and the damp air had ruined her hair.

For what? She'd been here less than a week, but so far her plans to meet boys were a near fizzle. Some other time, she might try a different approach with Nathan Webb. She decided he was worth the effort. It was a big *if.* Because if she had to razzle-dazzle him with dull politics, then he wasn't her man.

The pickings ought to be great, so many guys. Something would happen, soon.

Chapter Six

Hillary had found inn doings—meals, maids' cleanup, and the coming and going of guests, permanents and overnighters—predictably dull. Only work in the shop kept her from being bored silly. By the second week, she preferred to be there more than anywhere else. Guys came in, to buy greeting cards, paperback books, souvenirs for home, and to flirt. Flirting didn't hurt, she decided, and for sure it added pizzazz to otherwise dull days. She watched for Mr. Right to walk into the shop and planned how to know *him* when he did.

From the start, Abby's children were two regulars to the gift shop. The blond, big-eyed moppets were sometimes in her way. They never bought anything. But Hillary couldn't tell them to stay away, because she liked them. Keegan was a small bundle of equal parts solemnity and eagerness, thin-faced like his mother. His little sister, Kirstie, was a happy little thing whose moonbeam face often showed traces of her last snack.

Abby was still swallowed up in her own problems,

and the grandmother didn't seem to care that the kids wandered from home, even though Keegan was only five and Kirstie a year or two younger. Once Hillary asked, as Keegan quietly herded his little sister into the shop, "Doesn't your grandmother worry about where you are? Did she tell you it was all right for you to come here, downtown?"

"Gramma doesn't like us to bother her when she wants to take a nap," Keegan answered, "or when she's watching her soaps on TV."

"She says we can come here," Kirstie piped. "But Gramma says, 'Don't break anything 'cause I don't want to pay for it.'"

"Hmm," Hillary sighed. "You cross streets and everything, alone?"

Keegan nodded. "I'm careful. I watch the cars."

So cute and innocent. If she hadn't felt sorry for Keegan and Kirstie, she'd have refused to be their unpaid babysitter. But she felt bad because she couldn't tolerate their mother's dismal personality. And so she sort of felt she should do something for the kids. Besides, she was reminded of herself before the Germaines adopted her.

Hillary cleared a spot for Keegan and Kirstie in the back corner of the shop and supplied them with paper and colored pencils. Other times, when the shop was empty of customers, she would take a gift book from a shelf and read aloud to them. Like little sponges, they soaked up the attention. The open adoration they gave her in return made her feel wonderful. She began to feel like a protective mother hen toward Keegan and Kirstie Ross. A new feeling, because she'd never had much to do with young kids before.

Meanwhile, she found that there was more to running

even such a small shop than she had earlier thought. More than just being nice to customers, take their money, put their purchases in a bag. She explained it to Lei Haffner one evening when they met for Cokes at the Taffy Shop. "I have to keep records like you wouldn't believe. I make out sales slips for each item. Count cash at the end of the day, and then it's my skin if that doesn't balance against the receipts. Everything has to be written in a big ledger. Some days it's a mess. But I do my best. I have to make deposits at the bank and make sure the deposit slip is kept with the summary of sales, and—"

"Ick." Lei made a face. "I'm lousy at math, myself, business stuff. I doubt if I could do it." Her straw rattled suddenly in her empty glass, and she pushed it aside.

"I think I like it," Hillary admitted. "And I'd die from boredom without the job. Guys from the plant are coming around more and more. Aunt Fay says it's *because* I'm running the shop now. She doesn't mind taking their money, but she gets mad if she thinks we're noisy. 'Fooling around,' she calls it."

"She's probably forgotten if she ever liked guys."

"There's Ed Tandy," Hillary said with a shrug, grinning. "He's her 'beau.'" Her mind went back to the shop. "I especially hate it when Aunt Fay criticizes me in front of customers," she told Lei. "One day I decided to revamp some things around the store. My dad is a retail businessman so I know a few things. One day I cleaned up the shop. Dusted, vacuumed, and I made cute new signs, using my art stuff, to replace the dirty, old, worn signs. I moved slow-selling items up front and arranged them so they'd be more eye-catching—"

"And your great-aunt found fault with that?"

"No," Hillary admitted. "It was the incense and

floating candles that freaked her out. She swore I was trying to burn down the inn. But I've seen the candle thing done other places. I remember a boutique in Iowa that had floating incense and flickering candles all over the place. I decided to activate a little initiative and do the same here. It gave the place drama. The candlelight made the glassware glitter; it was class. But Aunt Fay threw a fit. I can't win."

"Bad scene, huh?"

"The worst." She was silent a moment. "I guess the old place is as dry as a tinderbox, and I shouldn't have done it. I didn't think. But Aunt Fay might have used more tact when she spouted off. That cute red-haired guy —you may have seen him around town—Cary Blake, was there. He's so neat. Several times I've seen him on the school playgrounds teaching a bunch of little kids how to play baseball. You could see he's very good with them." She was thoughtful a second or two. "Anyway, as I was saying, I wanted to die when Aunt Fay got on my case in front of him."

"I would have, Hillary! What did you do?"

"Nothing much, then. Except to put the candles out like a good girl. I think Cary was about to ask me out, but Aunt Fay scared him off with her ranting. Maybe he'll try again, I don't know." She shrugged. "After he left, I told Aunt Fay how I felt, that I needed a little breathing space. We've gotten along better since then."

That night, in bed, Hillary lay thinking about Aunt Fay. Maybe, if she, Hillary, were in constant pain, too, she'd be just as touchy and snarly. It must be terrible. A good thing the surgery was next week. That would stop the pain and maybe her disposition would improve. In the meantime, maybe she could try harder to see Aunt Fay's side of things. Do what she could to make the best of this fiasco. It couldn't hurt. And maybe her time here would go smoother. Then she'd be free to—do what? Right now she didn't know what. She felt lost. Her future loomed like a dark and foggy forest ahead. The thought scared her, and she tried putting it from her mind by counting sheep.

～

SHE'D ASSURED AUNT FAY SHE WOULDN'T RUSH TO date, but the prospect became more tantalizing daily. She might as well try dieting in a French pastry shop. Besides, how did you get to know a person if you didn't go out with him? Few girls got an opportunity like hers. And dating would help take her mind off Mom and Dad —what they'd done. Anyway, nobody could resist forever guys like Jordan Lafayette, for example.

Jordan had come into the shop maybe three times. He seemed to write a lot of letters, buying stamps and stationery by the stack, although she suspected it was more to see her that he came. She remembered him easily from one time to the next because of his impeccable manners. But then, he was also solidly built, brown-haired, about nineteen—only perfect.

One afternoon, the subject of roller skating came up between them. She told Jordan how much she had loved to skate, in Iowa.

"I'll take you skating," he said quickly in his deep baritone voice. "I'd like to very much."

"All right." She smiled, anxious for an evening of simple good fun. "Does Reesville have a rink?" She couldn't remember seeing one.

"We'll go to Salem," he said. "Tomorrow evening?" As though struck with an interesting new thought, he changed his mind. "No, let's make it Friday night. I'll pick you up here at seven."

Hillary couldn't help being excited, though she tried not to show it. In Iowa, her dates had been mostly in bunches. Going with friends to see a game, to go to a dance, or to a party. Launching her social life in Reesville with gorgeous guys would be momentous. History-making, even, she thought with an inward giggle. She would keep a diary…

On Friday, Jordan arrived in his parents' Mercedes, which, he told her, he had driven to Eugene to borrow for this date, the night before.

"I love it!" she told him. The Mercedes was a bit fancy for a skating date, but was the sort of neat, crazy idea that kept life interesting. *Any more surprises, Mr. Lafayette?* she wondered silently, smiling at him.

As if on cue, clasping the steering wheel, he asked, "Would you like to go to dinner, first?"

Bummer. She'd thought the idea was just to go roller skating. She'd already eaten. But maybe she could fake it by just having salad and a light dessert. "I'd love to have dinner." She settled back, sighing. *Go for it, Hill*, she told herself, *go for whatever*.

Their conversation on the way to Salem was a bit self-conscious at first, then became an easy exchange. Jordan was a city boy, having grown up in San Francisco. He was an only child, like herself. In many ways, although they had grown up two thousand miles apart, their backgrounds were similar. Hillary relaxed, feeling very comfortable with him.

At the restaurant, she toyed with her water glass and

asked, "So how come you ended up in Oregon, Jordan? I can't imagine anyone giving up San Francisco for here."

He put down his fork, then explained, "A few years ago my dad decided he'd be happier out of the city, so he moved his business up here. He sells organs."

Hillary almost spilled her water. "Sells organs!" she exclaimed, aghast. Then she realized he must mean musical instruments. But she decided to tease, "Like for transplants?" she asked innocently, "hearts, kidneys, and so on. Like in the movie, *Coma?*"

He looked at her, not sure she was kidding. "Musical instruments," he said slowly, "like the piano."

"Thank God!" she cried. She burst out laughing.

"You can't imagine the first picture that came to mind —your father, an older you, standing behind a counter—" She choked with giggles, unable to continue for a second. "B-boxing b-bloody organs for customers—" Her voice died in a strangled laugh. Jordan was looking at his plate of veal marsala with an odd, sick expression. Jeez, had she ruined his appetite, being gross? He must think she was *dumb*.

Then, she caught the twinkle in his eye, and she knew he had been pretending. He picked up his fork and began slurping his food down like a werewolf at a human feast. It was sickening, but funny. Both of them laughed until tears came. Hillary's side hurt. "Jordan," she gasped, "you're terrible."

"You, too," he said. "Isn't it great?"

The skating rink when they arrived was a swirl of blinding lights, rollicking laughter, loud music, and the sound of whizzing skates. In seconds, they were a part of it all. Jordan was a polished skater, leading her expertly through the dances on skates in time to the music. She'd always loved to skate, but this was the greatest. For two hours they raced, spun, dipped, and swayed. Time flew, much too fast. It was a wonderful evening.

Hillary was yawning happily when they left the skating rink. By the time they reached the inn, she was asleep. "I'm sorry," she said, as she came awake and saw "Tara" looming in the headlights. She straightened from his shoulder where she had slumped and smoothed her hair. "I must have been more tired than I thought."

"No problem. My pleasure," Jordan said softly. "May I see you again?"

She hesitated only a second. "Sure." Agreeing to see him again didn't mean a trip to the altar. She'd get her chance at all those other guys. "Thanks for a very fun evening, Jordan. Night."

~

SHE WAS ALONE IN THE QUIET, CLUTTERED GIFT SHOP, rearranging a pile of cuddly bears, sorting Papa bears from Mamas, and so on, when a slim, dark-skinned guy came in a day or so later. She couldn't remember seeing him before, but right away she decided if ever there was a G.G., here was one. Her spirits took a leap.

Hillary remembered Aunt Fay's rule about allowing no food in the shop. So, after hesitating a moment, she told her customer, "I'm sorry, I-I can't let you bring food in here." Because she could see only the profile of his gorgeous face, she couldn't tell if she had offended him or not.

He unfolded slowly from where he was stooped, examining crystal paperweights on a low shelf. He looked at her with deep-gray eyes, questioningly, then at the bag of potato chips, sticks of red licorice, and bottle of soda in his large hands. It was as though the food was new to him, appearing by magic.

"You'll get grease on the merchandise, maybe," she explained lamely, "or spill the Dr Pepper—"

"I will?"

"No, of course not. But it's my Aunt Fay's rule." She felt her face flame. This guy was more than cute.

She was glad she'd dressed up today, in her mauve shell and linen skirt and heels.

He crouched and started to ease backward out of the shop. "I understand. I was looking for a little present to send to my mother. You pick something out for her. I'll take my supper and finish it out on the porch like a civilized man. Deal?"

"Deal. But," she protested, "wait a minute. I don't know anything about your mother. If you can give me some ideas, I'll pick something appropriate. Tell me about her?"

He sauntered back, his dark head barely clearing the top of the doorframe. Looking down at his shoes, he inched back a step so that he stood beyond the threshold, causing Hillary to smile. She waited while he munched a mouthful of chips and sipped his Dr Pepper.

"Well," he began, "like me, Mom is an Indian. Klamath tribe. Pa is, too. I wanted to buy her something special since I just got paid. Something she might not get for herself. The folks have a little general store down in the southern part of the state. They cater to sportsmen and tourists, and they carry a lot of this stuff in their store—" He waved an arm, clutching his food to his chest with the other arm. "And that isn't what I want."

"How about a good book, does she like to read? We have some new books, best-sellers."

"Can't read very well." He shook his head and nibbled at a chip.

"A pretty scarf, then?" Hillary draped one over her arm.

"Nah. She wouldn't like a scarf with a picture of a beaver and a map of Oregon on it. She knows where she is."

"I'm sorry." Flustered, not sure what to do, Hillary finally told him, "Look, this may take a while. Go outside and wait like you said." She could do better without him looking on. "When I've picked out a few things, I'll bring them out to the porch for you to see and choose from."

He held the bottle of soda aloft by way of answer and left.

She wanted to please him, badly, but how was she to guess what his mother would like? And further, what would satisfy the son? She rejected a painting of a wildcat on velvet, the myrtle wood lamps, and the crystal cake plate. A craft item, well made, might be best. Gathering a set of rag-rug calico placemats, a crocheted straw handbag, and a mouse-shaped wooden cheeseboard into her arms, Hillary went looking for her customer.

He rocked languidly in a porch rocker, a crumpled sack in his lap, the soda bottle standing empty by his chair. The last smidgen of red licorice was disappearing into his mouth. "Can I come in now?" he asked, brushing away crumbs. "I finished my dinner."

"Please," she said, "come inside. I brought these out to show you, but you may see something you like better."

As it turned out, he preferred the hand-crocheted

handbag. "Will you wrap and mail it for me, too? Please? I'm living with some guys in a tent, and string and paper is something we don't have handy around our little teepee away from home. I'll pay the extra."

"No problem." She smiled. "You must work on the Burton-Sipes project?"

He nodded, and stood there a moment. Then he rifled the pages of a paperback book he took from a rack. "Warm today, isn't it?" he said.

"Finally, hot weather! I think we've had enough rain."

"This is a crowded town, isn't it?" he mused. "With all the construction going on. Lots of workers."

"But not enough to do for fun, in such a small town, is there? This town could use a good theater, other things..." After that, they seemed to have run out of words. But he didn't leave. "Was there something else you wanted?"

"Well," he drawled, "I thought you might want Mom's address." He shoved a scratch pad that lay on the counter closer to her resting hand. "How about taking it down on that?"

"S-sorry, I guess I lost track—" She was behaving like a klutz. She had to stop. She'd forgotten to take his money, forgotten to ask for his mother's address, forgotten everything. Except his white-toothed lopsided grin that was settled steadily on her again.

"Make sure she knows it's from me," he was saying. "Tony Redstone is the name."

Forcing herself to write calmly as he dictated, she managed to put down, *Mrs. Gloria Redstone, Box* 33, *Fort Klamath, Oregon,* and the zip. A moment later, Tony Redstone solemnly returned to her hand the thirty cents too much change she gave him.

If the trash basket were only her size, she'd have jumped in and hid! Instead she stood stock still and gave him a stiff smile of farewell. The instant he was out the door, she grabbed her head in both hands, twisting it from side to side. "Eeeee!" she squealed, before leaping toward the window to watch his tall, dark, *scrumptious* body slide into a polished brown Camaro and drive away. He was such a dream!

And what a great impression she'd made on him. Oh, she was a real vamp, the femme fatale of Reesville!

She'd be lucky if she ever saw him again.

Chapter Seven

Hillary was determined not to waste any more time availing herself of Reesville's supply of males. But her dating campaign was temporarily sidetracked when she volunteered to drive Aunt Fay back and forth to the doctor's for some last tests before going into the hospital.

"Ed and me are just getting too old," Fay Renshaw complained on one trip to see the Salem doctor. "And I hate the idea of failing, being helpless, needing someone besides myself to look after me. You young ones have the best of everything, Hillary."

Sure, no worries at all, Hillary thought. She took a few seconds to study her great-aunt's face and she saw plenty of worry and fear there. "We have our problems, too," she said, doubting it would be of any consolation. "Being young isn't the perfect time of life as some people think. Too many people are sure that all teenagers worry about are pimples, proms, and the right clothes."

She tried to explain, "Aunt Fay, that just isn't so. We worry about nuclear war, you can bet. We know about death. We lose friends in automobile accidents. Or now and then to a life of drugs, which is—a kind of death. We think about God, a lot. We just hope we grow to be as old as—a lot of other people. We wonder about our future, what tomorrow has waiting for us—" Especially lately, *she had.* She stayed silent, embarrassed that she might have gone too deep.

"You're right," Aunt Fay admitted. "All of us humans have our troubles. And we should support each other however we can. I'm glad you're here with me, Hillary. Having somebody young and strong beside me gives me courage. I feel easier, more secure."

For a few seconds Hillary was so affected by her great-aunt's words that she couldn't reply. The coolness she and Aunt Fay had first felt toward one another was evaporating. She wasn't sure just when it began, but she was glad. Glad about the good feeling between them. Closeness. The very special vibes a person felt from family, and from no one else. As much as Aunt Fay needed her young strength, she needed her to be—her family. It was pretty simple, really.

Through a thickness in her throat she asked, "Are you worried about the surgery, Aunt Fay?"

"I am. And I'm not. I'm scared of being put under by anesthetics and not being positive I'll come out of it. I don't like the idea of being cut into. But I suppose those are foolish worries. Because at the same time, I'm happy that somebody invented these marvelous plastic sockets and joints they're going to give me. My old worn out hip joints will be replaced, and I'll be like new. And I'm darn glad these doctors know how to do their business with me asleep so I don't feel anything. Mostly, I'm glad, not worried."

"Good!"

"Take care of your health, Hillary," Aunt Fay said earnestly. "That's one thing youth does have going for it, good health. I could have taken better care of myself, and this might not have happened. I should have exercised more, been more careful of my diet. We pay for not taking good care of our bodies."

Hillary considered it a blessing that she and Aunt Fay were getting along. But it still surprised her when Aunt Fay declared Hillary was the only one she needed with her when she went into the hospital. She said she would feel better if Ed stayed home to help Mavina run the inn. Hillary felt rewarded, somehow, and proud of herself.

Two days before the scheduled surgery, Hillary took Aunt Fay to the nearest hospital, in Salem, thirty-five miles from Reesville, and helped her to check in.

Now, on *the day,* she had gotten up at five a.m. and had driven back to the hospital for a few minutes with Aunt Fay before surgery. The elderly woman, tight-lipped and waving shakily, was soon whisked away. Hillary felt lightheaded herself from nerves and fear.

In a while, several women, whom she recognized as friends of Aunt Fay's, arrived. Virginia Webb, Nathan's mother, attractive in a pink suit, told her softly that they just wanted to be there, a kind of silent "rally squad" to cheer Fay's getting through this. Then they would go.

"That's okay, very nice of you." Hillary smiled. They sat down across from her in a row of chairs. One of the women wanted to know how she was adjusting to life in Oregon. Feeling a tight uneasiness still, she answered something. The woman smiled and seemed satisfied. A couple of them took out some needlework, and they conversed with one another in low undertones.

Hillary got up and crossed to a table laden with magazines, picked up a copy of *Time* and returned to her seat. She leafed through the entire issue knowing nothing of what she saw and read. Only once had she spent much time in a hospital that she could remember. That was when Colby Danson hurt a kidney playing football, their sophomore year. She'd cried herself sick, almost, she was so scared he was going to die.

After a while, a nurse at a small desk in the waiting room looked up from some papers she was writing on. She spoke to Hillary, "You're here for Mrs. Fay Renshaw, aren't you? It will be hours before you can see her, you know. She's still in surgery, and she'll be in the recovery room for an hour or two after that. Perhaps you'd like to go home and come back later?"

"No, I'd rather wait." For one thing, the drive back to Reesville was too long, for the other she felt committed. She *wanted* to be here for Aunt Fay. She was family.

Sometime during the long wait, two of Aunt Fay's friends went for doughnuts and coffee, but Hillary made little effort to eat what they gave her. She read five magazines, one a copy of *Science News*. In it she found an article about genetic engineering, cloning, and she decided the subject might be a good one for a term paper, sometime in the future.

School. Where would she be going to school this fall, after her parents gave her the official word in September that she was now her own boss? Would she attend Abbott High, live her own life in an apartment there? Or should she go somewhere else? She would have to have a job, to pay her way. She wouldn't mind a job in an art store. Or teaching crafts to kids, maybe. There ought to be several possibilities, once she settled down to determining what skills she had that she could use.

Did money have something to do with Mom and Dad wanting to be rid of her? Maybe Dad's business wasn't the big success she had always believed it was; it might be that he was losing a lot of money in these bad times, and he could only support Mom and himself. No, that was too far out to be even remotely true. Dad's poverty-stricken childhood had made him an especially careful manager of money. And Mom had an income of her own from the farms her family owned. A lack of money could hardly be the reason they didn't want to keep her. Besides, even people like Abby Ross didn't get rid of their kids just because they had little money.

Thinking about Mom and Dad, she began to almost feel her parents' presence. Mom's eyes, unless she wasn't feeling well or was sad, twinkled with such warmth. At the most needed times, too. She'd like to see Mom, now, feel her touch, her hug.

How were they getting along without her? Daddy was so provoking at times, but she loved him. And he loved her. Back then, anyway, he had shown it in a thousand ways. Daddy's partner, Will Porter, one time declared in her hearing that Lawrence Germaine cherished his kid beyond good sense. He'd said that. And it was true, she was sure. So why were they doing this? Why were they keeping secrets from her? It wasn't just confusing, it was tearing her apart. They weren't being fair to her as a person, or as a daughter, if they really did love her.

"Miss?" The reception room nurse came forward with a quiet smile, interrupting Hillary's bewildering thoughts. "You're a member of Fay Renshaw's family?"

She jumped up. "Yes." She swallowed. "Yes, I'm her family. Is anything wrong? Is Aunt Fay all right?"

The nurse nodded. "Her doctor just called down from surgery to let you know that the operation went beautifully. Mrs. Renshaw is in the recovery room now. She'll be kept there until all her vital signs are stable. That could be another hour, or two."

Aunt Fay's friends had overheard. They came forward in a body, smiling, exclaiming in relief to each other. Now that they knew Fay was all right, they could go home, she heard one of them say. Another made arrangements for them to take turns coming to visit her. Virginia Webb placed a hand gently on Hillary's arm. "Can we give you a lift back to Reesville?" she asked.

"I have Aunt Fay's car." She shook her head. "I'm going to stay for a while before I drive back, but thanks." She liked Mrs. Webb. She resembled Nathan, in looks. The same naturally wavy, tousled-a-bit brown hair. Both of them had clear blue eyes that looked at you—sincerely. Her mouth was like his, too, gentle and full. But his mother seemed friendlier. Nathan came across as more serious, although she didn't really know him. She'd seen him around. But after that showery day when he acted a little bit interested, his attentions had been zilch.

As Hillary watched the women leave, she wondered that she was thinking of Nathan at all. What was one guy in an embarrassment of riches? Anyway, today she had other worries.

She asked the waiting room nurse, later, "May I wait in my great-aunt's room for her to come back from recovery?" At the nurse's affirmative nod, she set out down the hall. Going up in the elevator, she was thinking that if doctors and scientists had the knowledge to clone people—create human beings in a test tube, using none of the ways known to man since the beginning of time—then giving a person a new plastic joint should be easy. In fact, Aunt Fay had told her that reconstructive orthopedic surgery was very safe. And a lot of people had told Aunt Fay that she would count today as one of the luckiest days of her life.

Beside the empty white bed in Fay's room was a mammoth bouquet of yellow roses, from Ed Tandy by the card. A smaller arrangement of sweet peas and stock was from Virginia and Charles Webb, and Nathan. Before Hillary could settle herself in the wide chair in the corner to wait, a nurse's aide entered bearing two more flower arrangements. Later, she returned with a pink-blooming plant.

Aunt Fay did have many friends. So was part of the reason she and Aunt Fay didn't get along well in the beginning due to her? Truthfully, maybe she was a spoiled, practically useless city girl, then. And her own resentment at being here must have shown too clearly, she realized with embarrassment. But Aunt Fay had been a—never mind. Anyway, hard to get along with. For sure, it was a relief they weren't still battling; whatever the reasons why, it was finished.

It was noon before Aunt Fay, looking wiped out, was wheeled into the room on a stretcher by an orderly and a nurse. The nurse told Hillary, "You may have just a minute with Mrs. Renshaw, then we'd like for her to get some rest."

Hillary watched them get the old woman into bed,

cringing with feeling for her. Aunt Fay's face was as white as the hospital gown she wore and a sharp contrast to her inky-black hair. Hillary went over slowly, took her hand, and tried to sound cheerful, "You've got a brand-new hip, Aunt Fay. Isn't that wonderful? How do you feel?"

"Thirsty," she said in a weak voice. "Happy this one is done. They kept me in the recovery room longer than I wanted to stay. Some fuss about my blood pressure."

"I worried about you."

"Oh, you shouldn't have. I was in good hands. To tell you the truth, I didn't expect you to be here. I thought you'd go back to Reesville."

"Not me. I wanted to stay. Your friends were here most of the time, too. Quite a few ladies. They stayed until they got the news that you were fine. They'll come back to see you during visiting hours. Ed Tandy sent you the yellow roses there."

Tears welled in Aunt Fay's eyes as she looked at the flowers. "I'm a lucky old dame. Some of the nicest people in the world are friends to me. And now—now I've got you, too. Your mom and dad maybe shouldn't have sent you out here, when you hated so much to come, but I do hope you make the best of it. You might come to like the Northwest and Rainsong Inn as much as I do. I'd like that."

Hillary nodded. It was true she hadn't asked to be here. But more and more she was determined to make this summer mean something. "I'm going to try, Aunt Fay," she said huskily, a teary smile nudging at her face, while her self-esteem soared. "Honest. And I promise to do better in the shop so you don't have to worry about that. No candles or anything."

"It will be time for you to open the shop, soon—"

"I know. I have just enough time to drive back. I'll take care of things, take your place as well as I can. You concentrate on getting better, okay?"

"I have to. I only have a week and a half or so to recuperate with this new hip before they do the other one. I'm glad I can count on you, Hillary."

The first thing Hillary did when she got back to the inn was to put through a long distance call to tell her mother that Fay Renshaw had come through her surgery just fine. The cleaning woman said Judith Germaine wasn't home.

"Do you want Mrs. Germaine to return your call?" the far-distant maid asked.

"No, I don't think so," she said after a hesitation. "Just give my mother the word that my Aunt Fay is all right."

She had had three letters from "planet-home" (well, probably not her home from now on) since arriving in Reesville three weeks ago. Mom's letters were bright cheery things, still pushing her to be happy and enjoy herself where she was. Every line hurt. Her answers were short, maybe sounded cold, but she tried to assure them that she couldn't be happier and they didn't have to worry. It was hard to write to them, but then, nothing about this summer was very easy.

A FEW EVENINGS LATER AS SHE WAS GOING OUT THE door, dressed and ready to visit Aunt Fay at the hospital, she crashed into Cary Blake, who'd come to ask her to go somewhere with him. Hillary sighed with regret. "Darn. I have another thing I have to do, Cary. I'm driving to Salem—" Then she debated; she *had* been wanting him to come back and her dating schedule was filling up. Once she began, she'd been accepting more and more dates, with as many guys as she could. Not that she wasn't careful. She didn't go with just anybody. But she was having fun. If she wanted to see more of Cary, though, she'd better go while she could.

Chapter Eight

"You're taking off alone somewhere?" Cary Blake cocked his head, his blue eyes surveying her, his hands deep in the pockets of his white jeans. The lamplight in the lobby made his hair smoothly spun copper.

She wouldn't mind touching his hair…going with him…to the moon, anywhere…she came back to earth, shrugging. "Alone. But I really should go. I have to see my great-aunt—" she broke off as he suddenly took her arm and propelled her toward the door.

"Say no more." He held the door open for Hillary. "I'll deliver m'lady wherever she has to go." He winked. "And on the way into the hinterlands—whatever hinterlands are—we are going to get a whole lot better acquainted. I've waited long enough to get to know you."

She laughed in agreement. Cary led the way to a low-slung blue Corvette in the inn parking lot. Hillary looked at the car, then at him. "They say the car a person drives is an extension of their personality. Is that true with you?" The car was gorgeous and so was Cary, but she thought she'd ask, anyway.

When they were in the car, he answered, "I'm fast, sexy, and irresistible. Does that tell you?"

"It tells me a lot," she said, still laughing.

They were well on their way, the Corvette purring softly, taking them swiftly through the twilight-washed countryside, when he asked her, "So what about you, Hillary? All I know about you is that you came here from Iowa to help out in that big old relic of an inn. And that you're beautiful to look at—"

"You need to know more?" she teased. "All right. What am I interested in? Besides guys, of course, there is art, that is number one. I'm into books, I love to read. I like clothes as in 'fashion,' aerobic dance, and I love going to museums and plays, not just movies. I have a thing for elegance, in anything. Which may indicate I'm not normal, or I'm a snob, I don't know."

"So far"—he sounded glum—"I haven't heard much that we have in common." Then he brightened, "I forgot! I'm an elegant guy! What else do you like to do? We have to get together—"

"More? Okay. I like sketching, sightseeing, movies—oh, I'm repeating myself. I love to sunbathe, but sunshine seems to be a rare commodity in Oregon."

"I vote for sunbathing." He ogled her in comic, roguish fashion.

"Cute." He was a flirt, but she rather liked it, liked him. "I think we might see a movie sometime, if you want to. Now, it's your turn, Cary; who are you? Open up. All I know about you is that you're a friend of Stratton Smith's, that you work on the Burton-Sipes thing, you're from Seattle, I think, and your family may be rich unless Stratton was kidding."

"He wasn't kidding. But you don't want to hear about my folks' money. You want to hear about me, right?"

"That's right." When he mentioned his parents, there was a flicker of something, she thought—sadness, anger —that showed just for an instant in Cary's face. So, he had parent troubles, too. "I want to hear about *you*. Where do you go to school, for starters?"

"Easy question. OSU. Oregon State University. A sophomore this fall. I'm an oceanography major." He reached to put a hand on her knee, but she moved it.

"What else, Cary? What other studies?"

"Girls' anatomy is my real major." He leered teasingly at her again.

He was certainly persistent with his clowning. "Okay. Forget school. What do you like to do when you're not working and you're not studying?"

"I was trying to tell you—" he began, still kidding. Then he asked, "You really want to know?" He threw his head back and looked down at her from under thick, rusty lashes. When she smiled, he went on more seriously, "I like to play tennis. But I've yet to see a good court close to Reesville. I like to swim, water-ski."

"I love tennis, too. Tell me about when you were a kid?"

That brought silence, then he told her, "I was always pretty much alone. No brothers or sisters, Mother and Father busy. That's the tear-jerking truth." For a while she thought he wouldn't say any more, then he went on, "As soon as I was old enough, I got a job with the parks and recreation department in Seattle. I was surrounded, then, man. I'm pretty good with kids, teaching them how to swim, play ball, different games and stuff."

"Cary, that's neat. I've seen you in Reesville, at the playground with kids. I'd like to introduce you to a couple little kids I know, Keegan and Kirstie Ross." She was turning them into little craftspeople, like herself. But there was lots they could be taught that she didn't know how to do.

In a few minutes, Cary's brashness was back. Playfully, he told her, "I left out that I like to sleep late, with someone else when I can, and I like spacing out on cheap beer. How's that?"

"I'd guess a bit of an exaggeration." They continued to banter back and forth, and the miles were eaten up quickly.

"So where do we find great-aunty?" he asked as they drove into Salem. "Do you have to pick her up somewhere?"

"She's at the hospital, she's had some surgery. I guess I didn't tell you where I was going. Come with me, and I'll introduce you. Aunt Fay is kind of an interesting character, and she feels well enough now to sit up and be gabby. I'll treat you to a hot fudge sundae, after." She looked at him, hoping he'd agree.

"You lost me on the hospital part." He shook his head. "No go." He caught her hand and kissed it. "But later, we'll go for the sundae."

"Hmm, all right. You can drop me off then," she agreed. "But I'll only be there twenty minutes. Pick me up at the front door around eight-thirty. That's when visiting hours are over and they throw us out of the patients' rooms. If you want, you can just wait out front for me. Listen to the radio or something since I won't be long."

He nodded, grinning, but he looked as if he hated to see her leave, and the truth was she wasn't anxious, either.

～

AUNT FAY WANTED TO TALK. SHE PRATTLED ON AND ON about her progress, stitches that were healing already, what her doctors and good-looking young therapist said and did, and what the dietitians were providing for her to eat. She had learned an amazing amount about the nurses' private lives in such a short time. It was entertaining enough, but Hillary realized that Cary Blake would have been bored stiff. She was glad he was waiting outside.

It was closer to a half hour that she spent with Aunt Fay, but she didn't think Cary would mind an extra ten minutes waiting. Finally, she gave Aunt Fay a kiss on the forehead and told her she had to go. She dashed for the elevator, glad now that she could spend the rest of the evening with Cary.

But when she reached the street, neither Cary nor his Corvette was in sight. She stood there, waiting, wondering. This had to be a joke or something. She circled the block, expecting to find him parked around a corner. She felt like a fool when there wasn't a sign of him there, either.

Hillary's throat dried, and an uneasy feeling took over. She returned to the front of the hospital, leaned back against a huge redwood planter of flowers, and waited. What had she done wrong, if anything? Maybe

Cary'd gone somewhere for a Coke and didn't get waited on right away.

At ten minutes after nine he still hadn't come. Hillary watched some nurses go off duty, and others arrive. Her worry became a gnawing feeling inside. At almost ten o'clock an ambulance went screaming away from the emergency entrance, scaring her further. The ambulance returned a short while later with a pregnant woman in noisy labor. Not Cary. Hillary breathed a sigh of relief.

Should she find a telephone and call somebody to come get her? Something might have happened to Cary, but she couldn't imagine what. He wouldn't go back to Reesville, would he? And leave her stuck in Salem with no way to get home? That would be a very unfunny joke. If he was the practical joker he seemed to be...fear tightened to a shakiness inside her, and she waited.

Traffic lessened on the street as it grew later and darker. The cool of the night, on top of her anxiety, made Hillary shiver. She wished she had brought a sweater. No, the thing she should have done was to have driven herself.

Finally, at fifteen minutes after ten, the blue Corvette purred around the corner and drew to a smooth stop at the curb. Cary jumped out and walked toward her, grinning. "Have a good visit in this creepy place? Let's go."

She yanked her hand back. "Wait a minute, Cary. What happened?"

"What do you mean, what happened?" He seemed honestly surprised at her action.

She stared, incredulous that he could be so unconcerned and unaware of his thoughtlessness. "I mean, you were supposed to be waiting for me. I came out at twenty to nine and you weren't here. I've waited an hour and thirty-five minutes for you to pick me up. Just waiting. Looking. I don't get an explanation?"

"Cool off. Sure you do. I went looking for a Coke and ran into a couple girls. We got to talking, and they didn't want me to leave."

"Too bad for them that you did," she snapped, hardly believing any of this.

"Hey, are you *mad?* Look, I'm sorry, really. I lost track of time, but I'm here now. Let's go get that hot fudge sundae. Ice cream will cool your mad down." He leaped to open the car door for her.

How could he be so inconsiderate? It was unbelievable. She stopped gritting her teeth, but she still seethed inside as she got into the car.

Then she began to think that maybe it wasn't his fault altogether. She should have told Cary back in Reesville just where she was going, so he'd have been warned, since he didn't like hospitals. He had been wanting to have fun tonight, and for sure a hospital wasn't an amusement park. And maybe he actually believed he was doing her a favor, giving her extra time to visit Aunt Fay. He could have forgotten she told him visiting hours were over at eight-thirty. He'd lost track of time, no big deal. "You can have a sundae," she conceded with a sigh. "I need some hot chocolate, I'm freezing. Then I'll have to get back to Reesville." A bigger concession she couldn't make, not tonight. Not until she got to know Cary better.

It wasn't a date to put in her memory book and brag about, she thought, going home. But she was learning a whole lot about guys, and some about herself. She didn't care to be taken advantage of, or be taken for granted, as if she were nothing but a lettuce-head.

~

WITH A TOUCH OF INSANITY THAT SHE HOPED WOULDN'T be permanent, Hillary began to think that guys weren't everything, anyway. She was feeling a certain pride in her role at the inn even when she wasn't overjoyed about it. Aunt Fay was recovering better than expected at the hospital. The inn was practically running itself, with everyone pitching in to do their job and a bit more. Then came the morning that Mavina pounded on her bedroom door to hurry her downstairs. She had to take some guests for a *horse and buggy ride,* Mavina said.

"What?" Hillary whispered groggily, leaning against her doorjamb, half asleep. "Repeat, please?"

She squinted at Mavina and clutched her short terry robe closer about her long-limbed body. "Horse? Buggy?"

Mavina Immel stood there in the hall like a blocker for a football team, in her cook's uniform, plainly anxious to get this errand over with so she could get back to her kitchen. "We have some new guests this morning, overnighters," she said with exaggerated patience. "A kid and his father. They have an outdated brochure on the inn, which advertised that we give free buggy rides for guests. We used to do that. Fay loved taking folks out and showing them the town from her buggy, but she quit when her arthritis got bad. But these folks won't take *no* for an answer. They claim the buggy ride is the reason they stayed here. You'll have to do something, because I can't. Do you know anything about horses?"

"Well…" Hillary yawned, still believing none of this. "I took horseback riding lessons back in Iowa, if that counts. Wait a second," she remembered drowsily, "the stables where I learned to ride had a cart—and"—she yawned again—"the other kids and I loved playing with it. We drove an old horse named Roger all over the place." Her hair was a mess, she hated to be woken up like this, she wished that Mavina would just vanish. She closed her eyes, hoping this was a dumb dream, but when she opened them, Mavina was still there. She sighed, "Where is Aunt Fay's horse? I don't remember seeing one."

"Old Hannah is in some rented pasture on the other side of the barn. The buggy is kept in the bam."

"I remember the barn, I just don't remember 'Old Hannah.'"

"Well, you'll just have to take my word for it! Ed will hitch up while you grab a bite of breakfast. But hurry. Abby says she isn't feeling well and she won't be in until this afternoon. Howard is visiting his mother. One of the part-time waitresses is taking over some of his chores, but even so I've got a ton of work to do, and I can't take any more of these people nagging for a buggy ride. Such foolishness." She bustled off, mumbling to herself, something about a "cherry chocolate torte" being ruined.

That she was agreeing to this craziness was a revelation to Hillary, later, as she sat high on the buggy seat behind a brown mare. Ed guaranteed that she'd have no trouble driving Hannah, that Hannah was obedient and then some. She hoped so. Beside her was her young charge, a skinny little boy named Jeremy. The boy's large cowboy hat pushed the tops of his ears down, and he could hardly see out from under the brim. "Well, Jeremy," she said, holding back a laugh of humiliation, "this is it, here we go—"

To get the feel of driving the buggy, she tentatively

urged Hannah up and down the driveway below the deck, several times. The old horse proved as docile and knowing as Ed promised. Hillary was deeply glad that her friends were in Iowa hundreds of miles away and couldn't see her in this foolish contraption. She hoped none of her new friends saw her, either.

"This ain't a ride, we aren't going anywhere," the little boy complained. "Daddy said you would take me for a long ride, and I'd see neat stuff."

She couldn't hide down here behind the inn any longer. She sighed. "Your dad was right. And we here at Rainsong Inn aim to please." She drew her shoulders high and drawled in mock Western lingo, "Hang on to your hat, pardner. We're headin' west. Giddyup, Hannah!"

Wishing she were almost anywhere else at all, Hillary drove Hannah clip-clopping through the streets of the older parts of Reesville. Beneath them the buggy shook and rattled as they journeyed up one street and down another. If this boy, Jeremy, wanted to see the Old West, she decided, then the direction of the Burton-Sipes Electronics Plant being built was not the way to go. It was progress, modern. But sometime, she might take the horse and buggy by there and give all the gorgeous guys something to take their minds off work. She giggled, considering what their reactions might be.

She pointed at a long block of older homes set amid trees and flowering shrubs. "See those houses? People were living in them more than a hundred years ago. A long time. Can you count to one hundred, Jeremy?"

He shook his head, his hands gripping the buggy seat tighter as he asked, "Are those houses haunted? Do they got ghosts?" Hannah blew through her nostrils, making the boy jump.

"I don't think they have ghosts. Those homes look too well cared for, like their owners love living in them. If the houses had ghosts, I don't think people would be happy there. The houses would be more shabby and spooky-looking. What do you think?" She was getting so she talked pretty well with little kids, she thought.

"I think one of the houses has a ghost. But I don't know which one." He swiped his hand across his face, looking embarrassed as though he knew better, but he'd rather believe in the ghosts.

That was okay with her. They came to the eastern edge of Reesville, and Hillary told him, "Looks like the wide open spaces ahead, that's for us." She started to sing, *"Home, home on the range."* The boy began piping the words along with her. Still singing, they followed a country road edged with tangles of wild flowers, and then they started up a hill. She was delighted to see an old cemetery at the summit. An old Western movie she'd seen on television came to mind. "That's Boothill Cemetery," she said gravely, lying in her teeth. She drew Hannah to a standstill.

Jeremy jerked up straighter, shoving his hat back. He stared. "Nah, it isn't. The real Boothill is a long way from here, I know it is. My daddy saw it one time, on vacation. This isn't it."

Smart little kid. "Okay, you're right," she admitted. "This isn't the real, official, famous Boothill. But who's to say that there aren't a couple old dead cowboys buried there? There might be, you know." The outdoor air must be affecting her brain, for her imagination to carry on like this, she decided.

"There—there might be—" Jeremy agreed slowly, his voice choked with awe. "There might be dead, dead cowboys in there..." He stared dreamily at the graveyard.

Suddenly, she envied him, so quickly carried away, ready to believe. Ages ago, when she was small, she was like that. Able to switch into a fantasy world so easily. This kid was making her feel ancient and at the same time deprived. If she could just plug into a fantasy, she could forget everything, not worry about what she was going to do with herself. Unfortunately, she wasn't a kid and couldn't do that.

In a while she told him, "I think we better be getting back, pardner. It's about grubtime. Mavina made some chocolate fudge bars the other day. If we're lucky, there will be some left." At an intersection on the way home, a grumpy-faced pedestrian waited on the corner sidewalk. They faced a man behind the wheel of a car, and he wore a dull, deadpan expression. Seeing them approach in the buggy, both men came suddenly alive, grinning widely. Hillary and Jeremy, seated high behind Hannah, waved back. Jeremy looked so proud and superior to the rest of the world, Hillary laughed out loud.

After circling through the older section of town two more times, they trotted down the drive at the inn. Hillary drew up the reins and brought Hannah to a stop. She took a moment to rest her hand on top of the cowboy hat next to her. The sun-warmed felt wiggled only a little. "This ancient rattly heap we're in isn't a Camaro, and you aren't exactly a Tony Redstone or a Cary Blake, but Jeremy, I want you to know I had a good time today. Okay?"

She jumped down and went around to help him climb down. He gave her a quick, empty-toothed grin, and then he scampered off to where his father stood talking to Ed Tandy, who was clipping faded blooms in the rose garden.

"I saw where some cowboys are buried, Dad." Jeremy's voice floated back to her. "It was just like on TV. I think they had a shootout or something."

Hillary gave an exhilarated sigh. She wasn't joking when she told Jeremy she had fun. In fact, it might be neat to keep it up for a while; maybe she could become Reesville's official buggy tour guide. "Mr. Tandy"—she cupped her hands around her mouth to call—"would you come help me unhitch?" She could rub Hannah down herself, she'd learned that back east. And she'd pick up the rest, hitching and unhitching, from Ed.

ONE MORNING, HILLARY FOUND KEEGAN AND KIRSTIE, Abby's little ones, sitting in the gravel at the foot of the drive, slowly filling their laps with rocks. "What are you doing?" she asked, half laughing as she stared down on their cottony heads, so intent in play.

Keegan spoke first, squinting an eye against the sun. "We're putting rocks in our laps to see how heavy they get." Carefully, he added another to the pyramid in his lap.

"Oh, well. I've never done that, myself. Sounds interesting." She kept her face straight.

"It is interesting."

"We done it lots of times," Kirstie added solemnly.

"Look—when you kids finish with your experimenting, how would you like to go for a horse and buggy ride?" They pawed the rocks away and scrambled to their feet, dirt and gravel falling, and raced to catch her hands.

It was gratifying, to say the least.

For the rest of the week, Hillary gave buggy rides, often taking the Ross children as passengers. She even convinced otherwise reluctant guests to go with her for a tour of the town. Unless they requested it, she avoided the site of the Burton-Sipes building project. When they did go by, she gathered her courage and waved back at the guys she recognized. They might wonder if she was out of her mind, driving a horse and buggy filled with tourists, but what the heck, it didn't hurt.

THE DAYS FLOWED ONE INTO THE NEXT, BUSY DAYS. Besides the buggy tours, there was the shop to run, the registration desk to keep an eye on. Dating as she never had before this strange summer kept her mind off her parents. She was having more fun than she would ever have dreamed possible. Going everywhere; no special tie to any one guy, and no demands. It was ideal, the way dating ought to be, she thought. Mostly she had fun. But not always.

Chapter Nine

"Joe Castleberry," Hillary wrote in her diary of a date one night, *"is into photography. Which is all right, I am too. But photography is all he knows. The guy is so wrapped up in himself and his genius with a camera, he's like a tight roll of film! You can't reach him about anything else. The entire evening, he didn't ask a question about me, not one. Someday, this guy may learn to share, to relate to others, but I think we'll both be middle-aged by then."*

She wasn't sure why it seemed so important to record this summer in her diary. But she did feel better after spilling her feelings onto the little white pages. And what she was learning about guys this summer might as well be set down, she thought, as beacons for the future!

Another night she wrote, *"Tonight I went out with Steve—can't remember his last name. We could have had a wonderful time, we saw a great movie. But when we talked, DISASTER. No matter what subject I brought up, this Steve person had a sarcastic opinion of it. His idea of a sense of humor, I suppose. At first I wondered why he asked me out in the first place, he was so condescending and cynical. It didn't take much to realize that this is his nature. Lose him."*

On the other hand, like Jordan Lafayette whom she'd seen a time or two more, many guys were nice on a date and a lot of fun. She recorded of Jim Field: *"Jimmy looks like he could be John Denver's younger brother, wire-rimmed glasses, wide smile, everything. And he likes so many of the same things I do. But especially art. This Sunday he took me to a Salem Art Festival, held in a big park. We talked ourselves hoarse, ate scads of ethnic foods, and saw so many beautiful things together. Yay for Jimmy, he's a friend to keep."*

Once in a while, she went swimming or cycling with Lei Haffner, and another time they drove miles to go shopping at a popular Portland mall. Lei wasn't like any of the girls she'd known in Iowa. But she was enjoying her more. Lei was a good friend in a time when every close friend she'd ever had was far away, and it helped.

Hillary visited Aunt Fay at the hospital as often as possible, glad that Fay's second operation was over. She would be coming home before long.

On sunny days, when Hillary had time to relax, she took a book to read and she sunbathed on the back deck. A few times, she caught sight of a lean, dark-haired boy down by the river. *Nathan Webb.* Exploring, fishing, she wasn't sure what he was doing. She had practically given up trying to figure him out. She didn't want to feel spacey over him if he wasn't interested. And anyway, her social life was hectic enough. They waved at each other, but neither ever moved to join the other.

She sketched. Drawing flowers had never before been an interest, but she found the flowers in Oregon exquisitely beautiful, especially roses. They demanded recreation with pastels on paper.

Writing letters home was still painful. She still felt tossed aside, discarded like a scrap of paper herself, by the two people she loved most and had always counted on for their love. Many letters ended in the wastebasket.

Business in the shop left her foot-sore and weary at closing time, but she always managed to revive in time for a date. Ed Tandy claimed, "Every young squirt in town has traced a certain pretty little buggy-driving brunette to this place." It was true that the majority of her customers were guys. They came in twos or threes, or sometimes alone; flirted with her, bought an item or two, and ended up as often as not, asking her for a date.

Sorting out her observations, deciding who were the spaceheads she didn't want to see and who were the nice, reliable guys she would enjoy being with, was an absorbing task. She was getting to know a few guys very well.

Not Cary Blake that well, she was reminded one late afternoon when he came into the shop. She still regretted that their evening drive to the Salem hospital had gone badly. Today he must have come to the gift shop directly from work because he still wore his work clothes. She knew something was wrong when he slapped a letter pad and a packet of envelopes onto the counter without a word to her.

She wrote the items on a sales slip and cautiously asked, "Got a problem?" Considering the dark hurt in his face, it was a brilliant question. "Cary," she tried again, "what happened to make you so down?"

"Nothing new." He made no attempt to return her smile. He shook his head. His face was flushed, his expression imploring. "Parents! Why do they bother having us in the first place? If they can't take one lousy weekend out of their 'busy schedule' to see us?"

"Uh-oh, parent trouble." With a look, she invited him to continue.

But he paced, saying nothing. Then, he finally told her, "I planned to go home this weekend to Seattle. To see my mother and father—a little family togetherness, you know? But today I got a letter..." He yanked an envelope from a back jeans pocket, waving it. "They won't be there, my mother says. She's going to San Francisco on an art-buying trip and my father has an important meeting with his 'heating and cooling' buddies in Olympia."

The last puzzled her. "Heating and cooling?"

His expression was explosive. "My dad is Big Guy for the Northwest's biggest chain of heating and cooling concerns. You know. Electric heat, air conditioning? But it doesn't matter." He drew a deep breath. "My mother decorates interiors. Our house is perfectly cooled, perfectly heated, fantastically decorated—and empty. A tomb, that's what it is."

"I'm really sorry, Cary. I can understand how you feel, but—"

"No, kid, I'll bet you don't. A person can tell by looking at a sweet girl like you that you've got regular parents who care a lot."

So what did he know? Here she was without parents' support or anything else, about to go down the tube; but at least, she was trying.

As he watched her, Cary's expression neoned from defeat to a wistful grin. "I will however give you the opportunity to cheer me up. Pizza and a movie, Saturday night? We didn't get to have that regular date. How about it?"

How could she possibly turn him down, looking the way he did, so miserable? "Sure, Cary, it's a date. Can we double? I'd like to take my friend, Lei, too." That'd make it double the fun; but besides, she still wasn't too sure of Cary, yet.

He agreed, "I've got a buddy, Dave Bellah, who'll go with us if Stratt can't. Pick you two up, at seven?"

"Seven," she answered. He started to leave without his package of stationery. "Here you are, don't forget this."

He came back, his hands running through his auburn hair. He took the sack from her hand, leaned over the counter, and dropped it—a direct hit—into the wastebasket. "If they don't care, why should I?"

"Cary, let me give you your money back!" she called, but he only waved, grinned at her over his shoulder, and kept going. She felt a further rise of pity for him. The boisterous, little-boy charm must be a front for a whole lot of insecurity.

A few days before, her own mother had sent her a new camisole top and a pair of designer jeans (consolation gift for the abandoned?), and Hillary decided to wear them on her first real date with Cary.

On Saturday night, Leilani showed up just before seven, breathless, looking adorable in a red shirt and army pants. When they went downstairs to the lobby, the guys were there waiting for them. With Cary, looking sporty in navy and white, was a stranger, not Stratton Smith. This new guy was blondish, not much taller than Hillary, and he had an engaging smile.

Cary sidetracked her from examining his friend any

more when he whistled softly at her and came to take her hand. She wondered if Cary'd been drinking when she thought she smelled beer. It was very faint, though, and he looked totally sober.

"Dave," Cary said, "this is Hillary. Hillary, Dave Bellah."

"Hi, Dave. I want you guys to meet my friend, Leilani." At Lei's frown, she corrected, "Lei." She told Dave, "It's easy to guess that you're part of the Burton-Sipes' crews. You must work outside all day, to have that awesome tan. I'm jealous." Lei's date was an eyeful. A trifle short, but his build was magnificent. That, and his dark tan and sun-streaked blond hair, definitely placed him in the gorgeous category.

"Hillary, Hillary," Dave repeated her name. "I have an aunt Hillary. She's a withered old lady. You don't look nothing like her, not like a Hillary to me, no sir."

She laughed and shrugged. "Just remember that I didn't get to name myself, any more than you did. Otherwise I might have been a Lori. Or Sharon, or Dee—or maybe a Wendy."

"I think Hillary suits you," Leilani told her. "You're pretty, you've got it all together, you're classy, and so is your name."

"Do I pay you your ten bucks for this arranged compliment now or later?" she joked from behind her hand.

As they crossed the lobby toward the door, Lei went on, "I got my name the craziest way. You want to hear it?" When they groaned in unison, teasing, she went right on. "I'm going to tell you, anyway. My folks were in Hawaii when I—you know, was conceived. Dad was there for his rest and recreation leave, this was during the

Vietnam War. Mom went to be with him. Once they knew Mom was pregnant, they just knew I'd be a girl. They started calling me, *Sweet Leilani, heavenly flower,* even before I was born. Ick! I'm glad I can be called just 'Lei.' That's a good name for a girl or a boy."

"If you're a boy, you fooled me," Dave said, rolling his eyes. Everybody laughed.

On their way across the porch, they passed Ed Tandy, rocking in a rocking chair. He grinned, and told them, "You kids stay out of trouble, hear? I don't want to have to give your auntie any bad reports, Hilly. I have enough trouble staying on her good side. If I had to take her the bad news that I allowed you to go out and get into mischief, I'd really be in trouble."

"It's all right, Ed. Don't worry—" she began.

"Remember the rules!" he interrupted, swinging a fist high.

Both Cary and Dave stopped in their tracks. "What rules?" Cary asked under his breath.

She whispered back, laughing, "I don't know. I don't have the faintest idea what he's talking about."

"He doesn't either, I'll bet." Dave grinned.

The foursome ran to Cary's car, the blue Corvette, and crowded in. Cary had affected a skillful British accent as he held the door for her, calling Hillary, "My pet."

Pip-pip'ing all over the place for much of the evening, he clowned a continued mixture of dignity and foolishness.

From the moment of Ed Tandy's remark and Lei's story about how she got her name, the four of them stayed on a natural high. Hillary thought they would laugh themselves sick at the hilarious comedy they watched at a Salem theater. Afterward, they gorged on pizza, and still later, had gargantuan ice cream cones at Baskin-Robbins. Living at the stuffy inn would affect anyone, she reasoned. It was no wonder she was behaving like a schizo, but she was having a wonderful time.

"Your limousine awaits," Cary told her when they were ready to leave Baskin-Robbins. "Bellah, old buddy, it's your turn to drive. Me and m'love get the back seat, pip-pip!"

They made the exchange. Dave, with Lei beside him in front, asked, "Where to, now?"

"Home," Hillary answered. "It's been super tonight, but I have to get back. My fairy godfather, Mr. Tandy, is probably still up, watching for me."

"Me, too." Leilani yawned. "I'm already late. I told my parents that I'd try to be home before twelve. Dad will be furious."

Cary clasped his arm about Hillary's shoulders. "You girls are kidding, aren't you?" He spoke with a trace of anger, surprising Hillary. "It's early, let's cruise for a while."

"Not for very long," she consented, squeezing his hand. "All right, Lei?" She'd hate for the younger girl to get into trouble at home. Parents were hard enough to handle without getting them mad at you. Besides, Lei was here tonight at her invitation, and she felt responsible.

Dave backed out and then gunned the car onto the highway, heading north, away from Reesville.

Lei sounded worried. "I suppose I can sneak in without waking my mom and dad. If they aren't waiting up for me. I hate getting them down on me; I could get grounded for weeks."

They drove in silence for a while. Hillary felt less comfortable in Cary's arms than earlier in the evening. Then, she had enjoyed his arms about her, at the theater and driving around to the restaurants. They had kissed once or twice, and while her blood didn't "boil" with passion, kissing him was nice.

But Cary was beginning to—grapple, paw at her, in a way that was turning her off. She doubted that Lei was having such a good time, either, now that it was past her curfew and she had that to worry about. Dave was older, probably nineteen. When they arranged the date, Cary should have told her that, or she should have asked. Lei was really pretty young for him.

She tried to pull away from Cary, feeling she was going to smother if he held her any closer. Enough was enough. She was beginning to think that she just didn't care for Cary all that much. She gave a small laugh. "Please stop. Be a good little boy."

"I'm not a little boy, that's the trouble." He nuzzled her ear for several minutes, then whispered, "Oh you—"

She slapped his hand and tried again to keep it light. "C'mon, guys, take us home." She strained to see out the car window into the blackened landscape that was bumpy and shadowed. They could be on the moon, for all she knew where they were. Dave had made several turns, she thought, and they had driven miles. "Dave, turn around. Please."

The car slowed and Dave spoke over his shoulder. "How about it, Blake, do we head back, take the chicks home?"

"No," Cary mumbled. "Not yet." His hand grasped

the back of Hillary's head and he pulled her uncomfortably against his chest. "The fun's just started."

"I want to go home," Lei wailed. "I have to go home."

"Please, guys. This is all very cute, but Lei and I have to get back. Let's turn around, go back to Reesville, now."

Like a belligerent child, Cary said, "My buddy Dave is the pilot. I am the navigator. You're both with us till we're ready to take you home. Be nice, loosen up. You'll get home sooner."

Hillary hadn't seen him take a drink, but she began to wonder if Cary and Dave hadn't been drinking on the sly. Or at least Cary. Or was he just naturally this obnoxious the longer he was on a date? She struggled to get away from him, but his arms were strong about her and his lips caressed her throat. "You've got the wrong girl," she stormed in a whisper, "if you're after what I think you are."

"A girl is a girl. They just need ol' Cary to prove it," he crooned in a way that almost made her stomach turn.

"Cary, let me go!" She twisted her face as his lips tried to come down on hers. "Get away from me!" In spite of her struggles, his lips found hers, dryly bruising them. She pulled away, panting, her voice catching on a sob. "Cary Blake, you're a waste of space!"

He threw back his head and laughed. Then he kissed her again, catching her off guard. One hand tried to slide upward under her arm.

"That's it!" She jabbed an elbow into his ribs, not caring if she splintered them. "I'm tired of being mauled. You guys are wasting your time. Take us home, now, or else."

"You've got me scared to death." Cary cackled. "Or else what?"

"What do you think, Blake?" Dave interrupted from the front seat. "This kid up here is about to bawl. Let's take 'em home, what do you say?"

"I say we go to Oregon City to look at the falls."

Hillary bit her lip, enduring the silence, waiting in dread for Dave to answer. He said, "You're the boss."

"No!" Hillary fumed. "You guys are idiots. It'll be morning before we get home again. Lei's parents are apt to kill her. Have a heart, use some sense. Let's go back." Of course, Cary felt if he kept her out long enough, wore down her defenses, she would give in to him. No way would she. Not tonight, not like this. Not with Cary Blake, ever. She had to figure a way to get them to turn this stupid car around.

It was her fault if Lei got into trouble with her mom and dad. She was awfully quiet in the front seat, huddled on the passenger side close to the door. At least Dave Bellah was decent enough not to force himself on the younger girl. But she was stuck with this pest, Cary. He murmured, his lips brushing her cheek, "Why are you giving me so much trouble? You like me, you know you do." His tight hold on her loosened as he ran his hands up and down her arms.

Hillary took the opportunity to draw away. "Cary," she said bluntly, "I did like you, do like you, but you're moving on me too fast. You're too rough. It may come as a surprise to you, Cary Blake, but you are resistible."

She felt him stiffen. "You think you're too good for me?" he asked. *Why did boys always use that line when they couldn't have their way?* she wondered. "Listen," he went on, "girls come on to me all the time. I have my pick of a dozen any night in the week. You're no better than they are."

"You're missing the point by a mile, Cary. This is our first real date. I'm not ready to let some guy I hardly know use me just because he wants to, get it?" She felt angrier than she ever had in her life before. "Take your hands off me. Move over. You're sweating all over me. You're taking the curl out of my hair—" She was starting to sound ridiculous but she didn't care. She was the boss of her body, nobody else. If Cary Blake couldn't understand that and respect her feelings, too bad. Let him think whatever he wanted. At least tomorrow she wouldn't have anything to be sorry for.

"The name 'Hillary' does fit you," he mumbled nastily. "I bet you end up a cold, old maid." He leaned forward to tap Dave's shoulder. "Keep going. They can go home when we're good and ready."

"Listen, Blake—" Dave started to argue, then he shrugged. "Okay."

For an endless-seeming time, Hillary stared out the car window into the night, fighting Cary's hands as persistently as ever. Only now he seemed bent on malicious torment as much as anything. Where on earth were they? She couldn't tell any longer which direction they were taking. She barely kept from crying in her frustration. Somehow, she had to get Lei and herself out of this, make these idiots take them home. How much the evening had changed, from the good time they had had earlier.

When she finally realized what she could do, Hillary was at first mad at herself for not thinking of it sooner. Lei's dad was a foreman out at the Burton-Sipes project. Cary and Dave probably knew who he was. What would

Lei's father do if he knew these guys were holding his daughter in this car against her will? She had asked repeatedly to be taken home, and they had refused.

"Lei," Hillary asked innocently, "what does your father do? Isn't he a policeman or something?"

Leilani's voice quaked tiredly, "No. He's a construction foreman."

"Where?"

"Burton-Sipes. I thought I told you that."

The reaction from Cary and Dave was even better than Hillary had hoped. "What's his name?" they demanded in unison.

"Ted Haffner." Lei sighed.

Dave swore under his breath. "God, Blake. I can't afford to lose my job. He's my direct boss. You work under Ted Haffner, too, don't you?"

"You know I do." Cary was silent a moment or two, then he went on, sagging against the back of the seat, putting his hands up behind his head, "Yeah, old Haffner is a workaholic SOB, just like my old man. But it would be my luck that he'd really be into 'fatherhood,' too, and give a damn about his kid. Hell, Bellah, didn't you get Lei's last name? Hillary probably didn't tell us who she is on purpose. Haffner'd probably kill a guy if he thought he was tampering with his kid's reputation."

"We're going back," Dave said flatly.

This time Cary gave no argument. But he continued to grumble that Hillary was no fun, cold, nothing but a tease, most of the return trip to Reesville.

She felt like hating him, but she didn't. She felt degraded and embarrassed, though. "Cary, I apologize if I gave you the wrong idea—" she tried once to tell him. But he laughed harshly, disbelieving, and she gave up.

She and Cary weren't suited for one another, but he didn't seem to care about that. That she was a girl, any girl, was all that seemed to matter to him. And of course he didn't want his enormous ego shattered.

As they neared Reesville, one desperate wish consumed her. She wanted to take a shower, crawl into her own bed at the inn, pull the covers up to her eyebrows, and sleep forever. And forget Cary Blake once and for all. She didn't have to put up with such stuff. There were other guys.

It was four a.m. and the inn was understandably silent as Hillary let herself in. Mavina, the only one sleeping downstairs since Aunt Fay was still in the hospital, she hoped would be too tired to wake and hear her. She crept up the stairs, her breathing checked, hoping that Lei had been able to get in, too, without being heard.

Chapter Ten

Her hassle with Cary wouldn't leave Hillary's mind, and tears filled her eyes as she got ready for bed. Just because he wasn't on close loving terms with his parents, it didn't mean he could take affection from a girl.

It might be true that other girls enjoyed his rough, macho maneuvers and would be thrilled to make love with him, but she doubted it. For herself, she only knew that she preferred a relationship to take some time, to grow slowly. From first getting to know a guy, to friendship and having good times together, and finally to love. That's what she really wanted.

She'd never thought that a simple meeting was all that was needed before going all the way. She didn't think so now, and she knew that was one thing she'd never change her mind about.

If she could just talk to Mom, tonight, about everything. But she couldn't wake her with a long distance call at four a.m., to say that she needed help. That dating, this whole business of making it on her own, was getting away from her.

Lei would probably get into trouble over tonight, but at least she had someone close by, to give a care. She, on the other hand, had to handle her own troubles in her own way as best she could. Maybe, she thought, if she could just get some sleep, she wouldn't feel so inadequate. Tomorrow maybe, she'd know how to cope.

A FEW DAYS LATER, HILLARY WENT TO CHECK ON LEI and found that her friend was grounded from even leaving the house for two solid weeks. The two of them tried to explain together that being out so late was not their fault, but Mrs. Haffner wouldn't budge. It surprised Hillary that a mother could be so stern. She'd usually been able to sway her parents with such an open discussion. In the end, Lei had no choice but to finish out her two weeks' isolation.

It was so depressing, Hillary considered putting on hold her own dating, but that seemed a little extreme. After all, she'd had only one really bad experience. Nevertheless, her summer quest to find a special someone was going badly, she decided, and wondered how to improve it.

One afternoon, Nathan Webb came into the gift shop. She'd never seen him anywhere but outdoors, and it seemed odd to have him here among the gift shop's potpourri of goods. With his jeans, he was wearing a blue plaid shirt that made his eyes all the bluer. She felt something outdoorsy about him, as though he had brought the sunshine and fresh air inside with him. Her heart, for no good reason, quickened its thumping.

She finished with a customer, a woman buying a batch of greeting cards and pens, then she turned to Nathan. He was watching her. "Hi, how can I help you?" she asked him.

"Mom wanted me to pick up a package for her, something she ordered by phone?" He cleared his throat and then looked into her eyes for the briefest second.

"Oh, sure." She spoke casually, smiling, hoping to put him at ease if shyness was his problem. "Your mom ordered a pewter picture frame she wants for a friend back east. I'll get it." She dove for the package stored on a shelf below the counter. "Your mother is one of our best customers," she mumbled up to him as she rummaged through the sacks, looking for the right one. "And Aunt Fay certainly appreciates Virginia visiting her at the hospital."

"How is Mrs. Renshaw? I was in to see her a couple times, but I haven't got to see her lately."

"Oh, she's doing beautifully. Both hips are fixed now, you know. She gets to sit in a rocking chair two or three times a day, for a half hour or so. And the physical therapist has her walking and even climbing a few stairs."

"Hey, that's great."

She came up with the package and she held it out to him. He fished in his pockets, and a blush spread from his firm jaw to his shining blue eyes. Something was wrong, she realized, waiting.

"I'm clean," he told her, embarrassed. "Tom and Jerene, my kid brother and sister, have been in my pockets and ripped off my cash. They do that once in a while. I'll have to go home and come back." He swallowed. "I'm sorry."

"Don't be sorry. And take the package with you. I know Aunt Fay would trust you to bring the money another time, and I do, too." In fact, she was glad he'd come today without money. Now he would have to come back. She would see him again and maybe they could talk.

~

THAT EVENING, AT THE HOSPITAL, SHE ASKED AUNT FAY about Nathan.

"Interested, hmm?" The woman smiled from where she sat propped against pillows in bed. "About time you two took notice of one another. In my opinion Nathan's a genuine prize. Sure, he's a loner, and quiet, but he's got an awful lot going for him. He'll be somebody, someday, I'll vouch for that. He's got the makings. You see, Nathan cares a lot about—oh, so many things are important to him. He *cares*. You don't see young men like him, often. I chat with him whenever I can sit him down. With the right education, Nathan can fight back against the spoilers."

"Spoilers?"

"You know what I mean. Companies, industries, and individuals bent on ruining the land, or at least not giving a hang if they do. Already the boy is a walking encyclopedia about plants, wild animals, geology, waterways; you name it. I once heard him say that Tom McCall was his idol. Tom was our governor and loved Oregon so much and fought hard to preserve it against ruination."

"I've never really gotten to talk to Nathan," Hillary

said. *Because he's shown so little interest in me,* she added in her mind.

"Get to know Nathan, Hillary, and you won't be sorry." She nodded in agreement. But Nathan could make it easier.

In a moment she said, "There's something else, Aunt Fay. A lady named Ada Twigg called. She said she and her husband had written a book together, and-"

Aunt Fay cringed as though something had been thrown at her. "I forgot! Didn't I? Oh, those dear souls. I promised I'd give them an autograph party the minute their book came off the press. But that must have been last month. I've had so much on my mind. Ada and Morley Twigg are good friends, too."

"They hadn't known that you went into the hospital for surgery. Mrs. Morley said to never mind, but I told them you hadn't forgotten, that the autograph party is still on and I'm in charge. If it's all right with you."

Aunt Fay stared at her, speechless, but her eyes sparkled with feeling.

"I said I'd take your place," Hillary told her. And she was still determined to prove to others that she was *not* Miss Useless of the Year. Besides the autograph party, there were other things she'd like to try, but she would bring them up later. "What's their book about?" she asked Aunt Fay with a smile, hoping it was a romantic novel. It would be fun to meet authors of a book like that.

"Oh, it's a fine book, all about Reesville's Victorian houses and the history of the town. Nobody knows more about our town than those two do. I read some of their manuscript. It was good."

Hillary was momentarily disappointed. Then she said,

"I've never been to an autograph party, so I'm not sure what to do."

"Nothing to it. Although I've only given one, before, myself. For a young poet fella who was staying at my place. You just fix a table for the books and have a couple chairs for the authors. Easy as pie. Oh, you put a notice in the newspaper, too, and make a few signs so people know about the book signing."

"I thought about making it more of a party? Mavina could make cookies, we could serve tea and punch, I could decorate with flowers..."

"Whatever you want to do, child." Aunt Fay looked both pleased and comically flabbergasted. "Abby can get out the big old silver tea service and the cut-glass punch bowl. Sure, go ahead and make it a bang-up affair, anyhow you want to do it. I want these folks to sell a lot of books, Hilly, and I'll tell you why." She hesitated, frowning a bit. "The Twiggs didn't get a regular publisher to publish their book, you see. Couldn't find one who would do it and pay *them.* So the poor things took their savings out of the bank and paid a printer to do the book for them. Used every cent they had. They just have to get their money back, and I'd like you to help them do it."

"Consider it done." Hillary smiled quietly. Actually, an autograph party sounded like fun.

Next day, Hillary called the Twiggs. She automatically pictured them as two tiny stick people. So when they came to the inn that night to show her their book and talk about the book signing, she was surprised. They resembled whole trees more than twigs. Ada was big and rawboned, although her voice, by contrast, was as melodious as soft wind bells. Her corpulent mate drummed an accompaniment to his wife's greeting.

Hiding her astonishment, Hillary smiled and welcomed them, leading the way to a grouping of chairs in the corner of the lobby. The furniture creaked badly as they sat down. Quickly, she said, "I'd like to see your book; I've been looking forward to it." She reached for the volume that Ada Twigg held to her broad bosom as if it were a beloved child. She gave Hillary the book, smiling shyly and modestly.

On the cover was a picture of a beautiful Victorian mansion. But the title confused her. *"Bats in the Basement, Ants in the Attic?"*

In her velvety voice, Ada Twigg explained. "Naturally it's the other way around—you'd find ants in the basement and bats in the attic. We thought turning the terms around would catch readers' attention."

"The title fits the book, too," Morley offered in a friendly growl. "It's a kind of upside down, backward hodgepodge of history and information. The only such book on Reesville, though. A lot of interesting facts in there that you won't find anywhere else."

"I'm sure." Hillary nodded, still smiling. "It's a beautiful book. I'm sure it's good. I can hardly wait to read it. About the autograph party, is Saturday afternoon all right with you? From one o'clock to five?"

They agreed, their round faces showing their gratitude. "We have a whole garage full of books, unsold," Ada confessed. "Cartons and cartons of them. We just got carried away researching, writing, and getting the book printed. It was an act of love, every stroke. But the day the truck pulled up and started to unload all those books —" She hesitated and shook her head. "…I wondered what we'd done. What we'd let ourselves in for. We wouldn't have bothered Mrs. Renshaw about it, if she'd forgotten, but we're glad for this autograph party. Every spare cent we had is in our book; it just has to sell."

Hillary felt a twinge of concern. Would they blame her if the autograph party flopped? She hoped not. "We'll see what happens," she told them. "That's all we can do. I'm going to put up some posters around town. And now if you'll tell me about yourselves"—she took a small pad and pen from her skirt pocket—"I'd like some information to give to the newspapers."

Intrigued, Hillary scribbled notes as fast as she could. Both Twiggs had been born in Reesville. Ada's family, she had been Ada Scannell before her marriage, had come to the area as pioneers. Her grandmother was a schoolteacher, and her grandfather, Ben Scannell, was an orchardist and farmer. Morley's ancestors came about the same time, newspaper folk. There had been Scannells and Twiggs from that time to the present, seeing every change that came to Reesville. In the minds of the Twiggs, the Burton-Sipes plant was the least welcome change. They agreed with most of the old-time residents, not the newer people in town, that Burton-Sipes never should have been allowed to come.

Hillary wrote on, fascinated by their personal stories; and yet, she realized with an inward giggle, she was going to have far more material than she could use. These particular Twiggs were going to need pruning.

She wasted no time getting started on the posters after work the next day. Using her own art supplies, she worked with precision, enjoying herself. For a proper effect, she'd settled on a bright watercolor rendition of the Victorian mansion and gardens from the book's cover as an illustration for the posters. She used black lettering to give the autograph party information and book title.

The third evening after their conversation, a boxed article about the Twiggs and their book party appeared on the front page of the Reesville *Times*. Hillary saw with satisfaction that her wording of the story had been changed very little. She just might combine writing with her art, someday. It was something she should consider, she thought.

Mostly, she was pleased that the newspaper editor chose to give the autograph party such prominent notice. They needed all the help they could get. The editor must know the Twiggs well and like them as much as Aunt Fay did. Although she had talked with Ada and Morley only the one time, she liked them, too.

In the giftshop on Friday, between customers, Hillary tidied up. She dusted, washed the one window, and straightened shelves. In conference with Mavina, she planned to serve large trays of cookies: fudgy walnut sticks, old-fashioned lace cookies shaped like tiny scoops, and delicate butter cookies. All from old-time recipes in keeping with the Twiggs' historical book. Abby would trade her uniform for a long dress, and she would pour lemonade and minted iced tea.

She still worried how many guests—customers— might come. A lot of the time she pictured the small gift shop swamped, but that might not happen. What if no one came? She'd had a birthday party like that in third grade. Of course that disaster came about because she was a little dumb bunny, as Mom said, and she had deposited her invitations in a trash bin instead of a mail-box, by mistake.

Hillary was just finishing her lunch in the dining

room on Saturday when the Twiggs came looking for her, almost filling the wide archway into the room from the lobby. "The famous authors!" she exclaimed, getting to her feet, hoping to make them feel more comfortable than they looked. Morley Twigg perspired heavily. Ada had penciled one eyebrow higher than the other, due to a shaking hand, probably. The crazy angle of her brow gave her a jaunty, devil-may-care appearance, put to lie by her quivery smile. "Everything is ready, except the books," Hillary told them, swinging away in the direction of the gift shop.

Luckily, she'd found two sturdy chairs. She had placed them just inside the gift shop by a pretty Eastlake antique table and had cleared spaces on a few shelves behind for baskets of flowers. Abby and another girl came now to the tea table just outside in the lobby with trays of cookies. Hillary went out, clasping her hands in delight, feeling proud. The table was centered with a huge bouquet of Ed's nicest flowers: roses, snapdragons, day lilies, shasta daisies, and fragrant dianthus. "It's all so pretty, so perfect," she chortled to Abby. The other waitress had gone.

But Abby responded little, and she felt let down. There were times when she thought Abby's depression, from the loss of her husband and the weight of her responsibilities, was getting worse instead of better. She smiled kindly at Abby, hoping to help her feel not so blue. Abby's return smile showed little real feeling.

Hillary was stumped. She wanted to do more, offer words of encouragement, something. But at the moment, the Twiggs needed her, too. They had been coming and going for some time, carrying in cartons of books. She sighed and went to make a few neat stacks of copies on the Eastlake table, standing a few on end so the cover could be seen straight on.

"We're ready for the book buyers!" she said brightly to Morley Twigg when he thumped a carton to the floor, narrowly missing her sandaled foot. On the next trip, she begged, "Don't you think that is enough books, for now?"

Ada, who had sagged into one of the chairs minutes before, said, "Yes, Mor, honey, stop bringing them in. You'll kill yourself if you have to carry all these back out to the station wagon."

"Oh, you won't have to carry books back to the car, I'm sure," Hillary bluffed. "In fact, I want to buy two books myself, right now. One for myself, and I'd like an autographed copy for my parents, too." If Dad loved this little town as much as he said, then he ought to appreciate *Bats in the Basement, Ants in the Attic*. Mostly, though, she wanted to put the party into action to bolster the Twiggs' morale. Their expressions were awful, as though they awaited prison sentencing as they looked out into the empty lobby. Along with Abby, they were some cheery group to greet possible customers, she thought with chagrin.

Between one o'clock and two, the Twiggs sold three more books. One to Abby, who behaved as if she'd sorely miss the money but wanted to do it if it was expected of her. Nathan Webb's mother, Virginia, happened into the shop to pick up a new photo album. She obviously bought the Twiggs' book as an afterthought, apologizing for forgetting about the notice she had seen in the Reesville *Times*. Hillary bought a third book, this one for her mother's mother back in Iowa.

Mrs. Coates came in. She seemed to relish the audience pinned helplessly behind the autograph table. She talked to them for a full forty-five minutes about the time she was stung by a bee as a child, causing partial paralysis in her left side. She didn't buy a book, but she thumbed one all the time she talked.

"Excuse me," Hillary told the three of them, "I need to check on something. I'll be right back."

She found Ed Tandy down in the backyard staking dahlias and cultivating around them. She explained that she knew he was busy, but she needed his help. He could use the rest and he could have some cookies and tea.

"I'll come right away, clean up, and buy a book," he promised with a wide grin. "I was going to, anyway."

Back inside, Hillary saw a woman she didn't know at the autograph table. She was buying *three* copies of the Twiggs' book. Hillary was surprised that she could feel such relief and thankfulness over the sale of a few books written by two people who were almost strangers to her.

The buyer said she wanted the books to send to relatives in other states, who once lived in Reesville themselves, long ago. Hillary watched with ill-concealed pleasure, almost dancing, as the woman bought a fourth book for herself, as soon as Ada and Morley had finished signing the first three. "I know my cousins will cherish these," the woman stated with a huge smile, "and I will, too. Everyone should have a copy. This is a wonderful book." She stroked the books covetously and Hillary wished more people felt that way. A lot more.

But the afternoon dragged on, hot and still, with only an occasional straggler coming in for a copy of the book. She felt awful, embarrassed for the authors, and somehow guilty, although it was hard to know how she might be responsible for the poor showing. It was hard to think of something to say to the idle, quiet Twiggs, much less look at them.

Abby slumped by the tea table, looking as if her life were wasting away.

Hillary hoped Aunt Fay wouldn't be mad at her over this. She knew she would be disappointed. But how could it be her fault? She'd publicized the autograph party in every way she knew how. Maybe people didn't want the book, didn't care about old homes or Reesville's topsy-turvy tales. "I think everybody is staying home where it's cool," she told the Twiggs. "Otherwise they'd be here in droves."

In the next hour not a single soul examined the books, although people came into the shop on other errands. Hillary would have liked to escape without another word to the Twiggs, but she stayed, smiling stiffly, sharing the Twiggs' discomfort and unhappiness, knowing the auto-graph party was a dismal flop.

At five o'clock the Twiggs exchanged a doleful look with each other and at her and began to pack up their unsold books.

"Wait," Hillary pleaded, "don't go yet, don't pack all the books." A guy had come through the main door and was crossing the lobby toward them. It was Stratton Smith, Cary's friend. He had grown a small dark mustache since she had seen him last, giving him a comic, romantic-villain appearance, except for his work clothes. "This may be a customer," she said softly to the Twiggs.

Chapter Eleven

eminded of Cary, Hillary's feelings hit a new low. But she had to put him and that awful date (mistake) out of her mind. Bygones being bygones and all that stuff, she thought, with a lift of her chin. "Can I help you?" she asked Stratton. His earnest woebegone expression was almost funny.

"Hi." Stratton sighed. "Sure glad you haven't closed up. I came straight from work. Actually, I took off a few minutes early. I got to have something neat for my mother. I got a telephone call from Dad, through my boss, and he's ticked off as hell with me. I haven't written my parents a letter"—he enumerated with his fingers— "I haven't called home to let the folks know if I'm alive, and now I forgot my mom's birthday. The jury is in. My dad's going to hang me if I don't shape up, pronto."

"Sorry about all that." Hillary already had a copy of *Bats in the Basement, Ants in the Attic,* in her hands. "But I think I can save you from the hangman. This book should get you off the hook." She held it out to him, and he took it in slightly grubby fingers. "It's all about Reesville, and it's very interesting. Reading the book would tell your mom all about where you are," she said quickly. "It'll be even better than a letter. And to make it extra special, you can have it personally autographed to her. These are the authors: Stratton Smith, I'd like you to meet Ada and Morley Twigg."

Relief flowed into Stratton's face as he examined the book. His mustache twitched. "Hey, you're right, this is perfect. Mom is into antiques and other old stuff; she'll love this. Sign it!" he exclaimed with a grin, passing it to Ada. "Sign it *to Juneann Smith.* And I'll write underneath, 'Love from your son,' stuff like that."

The Twiggs put their heads together, carefully composing an inscription in soft undertones. Stratton told Hillary, "I sure didn't think this would be so easy." He swallowed self-consciously and turned red. "Now, if the rest of what I came in here for works, I'll know for sure this is my lucky day."

"What do you mean?" She'd wondered if Stratton Smith would ever get around to asking her out. Now she wondered if Cary had told him something about her that stopped him until today.

He picked up a stoneware honeypot from a shelf and toyed with it. "I wondered—I came in to ask— I mean, will you go out with me?"

Hillary considered it, smiling warmly. Why not? The two boys were as different as night from day, even if Cary was Stratton's friend. Stratt was so open, she was sure he'd have no late night, backseat surprises for her. She glanced to see Morley finishing his signature with a flourish that brought his pen high, and an idea came to her. Wild, but maybe it would work. "Stratton, I'll go out with you on one condition—"

He leaned heavily against the counter. "You will? You mean it? Name it, Hillary, whatever you want, it's yours. Ransom? A kingdom? Heck, I'll go slay a dragon—"

"Never mind all that." Hillary giggled. She caught his hands between hers to make him listen. "I need a favor badly." She drew him away, whispering so the Twiggs wouldn't overhear. "Would you go round up a lot of the guys from the plant? Show them the book you just bought? Tell them the reason I told you for buying the book, and convince them that they should do the same for their families, would you?"

"Hey, that's all? And you'll go out with me?"

"Cross my heart. Actually, you'll be doing the other guys a favor, too. You'll save them from writing letters home, Stratt. Parents will like a whole book that tells about where their son is spending his summer." She nodded toward the Twiggs, who were beginning again to pack their books, "But you'll have to hurry."

"I'm gone!" Stratton leaped past the Twiggs, saying to them over his shoulder, "Don't put those books away. Don't move. I've got a hundred buddies who'll want a book like mine." He gripped the volume under his arm. "Give me a few minutes to go get the guys."

Ada looked startled, a shade disbelieving. But Morley pulled a stack of books back out of the carton and set them on the table, beginning to smile.

"You won't mind staying until six or six-thirty, will you?" Hillary asked.

Within fifteen minutes or so, they began to arrive. Still

in their work clothes, hair mussed, grinning tiredly, young guys streamed in a line across the lobby to bunch in the gift shop. Hillary hardly had time to speak to those boys she knew as folded green bills were shoved at her from many sun-browned hands. Making change and sacking the books grew hectic, the Twiggs couldn't sign fast enough, the room was crowded and warm. Too late now to hire Lei to help. She wished she'd thought of it sooner. "Don't go away," she urged them, "but do have some lemonade or iced tea and cookies until we can get to you."

She began to worry that Stratton had told the guys he'd won a date with her. And that he had given the impression that the same would happen to all of them if they bought a book. If he had, she was in trouble. With this many G.G.'s, she'd be dating around the clock. With no time to eat, sleep, or anything else. An interesting proposition—but impossible of course, she thought in a flurry. Whatever, though, she didn't have time to worry about it now.

Townspeople, attracted by the commotion, began to drift in, too. They milled about; one, two, and three copies of *Bats in the Basement, Ants in the Attic*, under their arm and a cookie or tea glass in the other hand. They conversed with one another as though glad for this reunion, this party. Hillary's mind spun as she tried to keep up with their questions and requests:

"Where are the authors? I want to meet them—"

"Will you send the authors to give a talk at our school?"

"—at our writer's club?"

"—to our business meeting and have them bring some books to sell—"

Once, she caught sight of the Twiggs through the

crowd. They were transformed, their timidity gone. They smiled, joked, or commented, before scrawling their signature furiously so they could go on to the next book buyer.

Either she was dreaming a fantasy, or this was a marvelous, book-selling boom. And she had done it!

Dave Bellah was in the line that reached clear back through the lobby and out onto the porch. When he drew near, he winked at her in an apologetic fashion, and he smiled. He bought two books. "One for my mother, and one for my aunt," he told her; then he added, "I'm glad to hear you've got a date with Stratt, he's a good guy."

Hillary nodded. "Nice to see you, Dave."

If Cary Blake was there, she didn't see him.

~

FEELINGS OF SATISFACTION OVER THE SUCCESS OF THE Twiggs' autograph party stayed with Hillary through the whole rest of July. It was a matter of bringing the right customer together with a product they needed. Maybe she had picked up Dad's super selling touch from him. In any event, she thought he would be proud.

Her life at Rainsong Inn was undeniably happier now. Inspired by Ada and Morley's book, she had taken to sketching Reesville's Victorian houses, hoping to collect them all. The day would come when these old houses would be no more, unless somebody, a group, took steps to have them preserved.

Art wise, she thought the things she'd done this summer were good. But if she wanted to earn an art scholarship next year, she'd have to be outstanding. No one else had seen her summer drawings, and it was only her opinion, but she was prouder of her work than she had ever been. In fact, she'd like to think of some way she could combine her art skills, her growing enjoyment of working with people of all ages, and writing, all in some future profession. She thought a public relations job of some sort would do, if she could qualify.

AUNT FAY WAS HOME FROM THE HOSPITAL. THE LONG trip to Reesville by car had been tiring and painful for her. It came to Hillary that it might not have been so bad if Reesville had its own hospital and ambulance service. Aunt Fay was still weak from surgery and took a nap each day. Hillary volunteered to help her dress and to get from her bed to her walker and vice versa. Mavina, Abby, and the maids, Eleanor and Patti, did their share, too. Even so, the elderly woman was healthier and more active than any of them expected she'd be. There was little doubt that she would be walking on her own, better than ever, before very long.

Among others, Hillary dated Stratton several times. They went to movies, and once in a while on a Sunday he accompanied her on buggy rides. He liked to take the reins and pretend he was an Old West muleskinner or some such. Now and then he came in the evening to play cards with her. They couldn't watch television since Aunt Fay wouldn't have a TV on her property.

Stratt was fun, and she was comfortable with him. But she knew that they would never be more than good friends. Whatever chemistry was needed for romance simply wasn't there. She guessed that Stratt knew it and that it was all right with him, too. They could enjoy one another's company, if nothing more.

But she felt guilty for wishing it was Nathan Webb spending time with her, instead of Stratt. Why did her dumb heart have to throb after a guy different from all the others? As far as she could tell, he had no interest in girls. Or was too busy to be bothered. She hardly ever saw him, at least not enough. His little sister and brother, Jerene and Tom, brought the money he owed her to the shop. In spite of herself, half of her watched for him constantly.

Then one evening, he did come by. She and Aunt Fay were on the back deck, relishing the coolness of the evening after a particularly hot day. Nathan drew his yellow canvas chair close to Aunt Fay's lounge, teasingly called her "Aunt Begonia," and apologized for being away so long. He'd been irrigating almost night and day, in the corn and sugar beets, he told her.

With a touch of envy, Hillary saw how comfortable he was with Aunt Fay. They talked several minutes, while she listened, about the usual lack of moisture from mid-June through September, causing almost drought conditions at times. *Even though Oregon was commonly considered a "rainy state"?* she thought.

"Son," Aunt Fay asked him, "have you checked out the riverbank this summer? I haven't been down there for months, to see what damage the winter's flooding might have done."

"Oh, he's been down—" Hillary began, then she shut up. Aunt Fay hadn't asked her.

Nathan's glance swept over her ever so slightly, then he answered Fay with a shake of his head, "I don't think you've lost much riverbank." He shrugged. "Oh, there was some damage, all along the riverbank, during last January's floods."

"Oregon's worst weather month," Aunt Fay agreed.

He nodded. "That's when almost everybody with land along the riverbank lost a tree or two, and soil."

Aunt Fay groused, "Why doesn't the Corps of Engineers send somebody down here! Do something about it! They could put a revetment along the bank, and that'd stop the erosion just like that."

What they were talking about was all new to Hillary. But looking at Nathan, the way his tan skin stretched smoothly over his high cheekbones, the clear clean gaze of his eyes, she wished she was an expert—at whatever he'd like to talk about. She clasped her hands in her lap and tried to concentrate on their discussion.

"They'd better not wait too long," he was saying, "or the river will take a lot more land. What most people don't seem to realize is that in time the river could take this town."

"Which might not be any worse than what's happening," Aunt Fay said. "I hear by the grapevine that Burton-Sipes may be trying to push some Reesville folks out. That the bigshots are trying to condemn some little houses, forcing their owners to move out to God-knows-where. That true? I hear some of the low-income families and some old folks on fixed income are nearly scared to death."

Pay attention, girl, Hillary cautioned herself. *We've now arrived at Reesville's favorite subject. Add something smart, if you can.*

She watched while Nathan seemed to gather his thoughts. "Dad says that the Burton-Sipes people would like to build some fancy condos and mobile home courts.

I hate to think the city council will allow them to push people out to do it. Some have been here all their lives and would have no other place to go."

Aunt Fay was very upset. "Tell me, Nathan, what does your dad think of all this? What's he going to do? I heard this boom is changing his place aplenty."

Hillary, listening, remembered that Aunt Fay had said Nathan's father, Charles Webb, owned one of Reesville's two nightspots, besides being the mayor.

Nathan looked grim and at the same time disgusted when he told Aunt Fay, "Some of the new people moving into town are rough characters. Dad's been robbed twice already this summer, and he's had to double up security. I used to sweep up for him. Now I hate to go near the place. Saturday nights are a mess—kids from the plant families trying to get in, claiming they're older than they are. They get sick. Fight. Then somebody calls the cops, and some of the kids end up in jail."

"What's it all coming to?" Aunt Fay shook her head. "Your dad always ran a respectable lounge. It's not fair that this had to happen to his business."

Nathan nodded. "He's thinking of getting out of it, trying something else. As mayor, he tries to be impartial and give the town what it wants. I don't think Dad, personally, is too happy about Burton-Sipes moving in here."

"Just a minute," Hillary broke in, honestly interested now, "I don't understand some of this. With all the new people in town, aren't the business places making more money? Getting rich, even. I'd think they'd be glad."

Nathan's chin lifted, and he gave her a long look. "Some are, of course. For others business is almost too good. Most merchants don't have enough help. Their employees have quit to take higher paying jobs building the plant, or in some of the other construction here. And when the plant is finally in operation, it could get worse."

"I doubt it," Aunt Fay said harshly. "I predict that the plant won't help the local people much as far as employment goes. You have to understand that those jobs will require skilled workers, well-educated in high-technology. Wait and see. They'll bring in outsiders for that, the best jobs won't go to locals."

"And"—Nathan sighed heavily—"that means the economy will then be geared toward those new, high-income residents. Inflation and more inflation." He raked long fingers through his hair, tousling it more than ever. "Isn't that right?"

"Wait a minute," Hillary begged again. "Will one of you explain to me how Burton-Sipes came to be here, if so many people didn't want them and still grumble?"

Aunt Fay nodded at Nathan.

He looked earnest, spreading his hands, collecting his thoughts to tell her, "It isn't really so complicated. Burton-Sipes directors' scouted around for a site for their proposed company, did some studies, and found Reesville suitable. The town is located between two large universities, there are recreational attractions for their would-be employees, this valley is a great place to live and a great place for a company to grow. They found someone willing to sell them the property they needed. That's it."

"But didn't the townspeople have a say in it? Didn't they get to vote or anything, whether they wanted Burton-Sipes here or not?"

Nathan shook his head. "There was plenty of input from every side. But the only ones actually voting were the six city councilmen. And it was a close vote, four to two. It turned out that a municipal bond was necessary to pay for increased facilities like sewers, streets, and other improvements. Townspeople voted on that—"

"Voted 'yes'?"

"By a small margin, but they did vote *yes.*"

Aunt Fay grunted in displeasure, as though the very idea was too awful to contemplate.

Nathan smiled at her gently. "The Burton-Sipes Company is funding some of the improvements, like streets. And a lot of people are working who weren't working before. We have to look at that."

Nathan was such a thinking person, different from most boys she was seeing these days. Aunt Fay was right. There was more to him than his outward, outdoorsy appearance led a girl to believe. She would like to add something significant to the conversation, herself. She thought back to what she had seen firsthand, the ravaged landscape of an otherwise pretty, peaceful little town. The long waiting lines of angry, impatient people at the supermarket because the store was short of help and customers were myriad. And the people who came to the inn, begging for a room when there wasn't a single vacancy left in town. The plant moved in and started to build when the town wasn't ready for it, that was the trouble. But maybe this was something every town had to go through, before things evened out, became better in many ways—

Too late, Aunt Fay had the floor, "We'll be taxed near to death to pay for all the new stuff, the so-called 'improvements' to the town. And the burden will be on the old-time residents. They've always thought of Reesville as their town, but they won't be able to afford to stay on. If they aren't condemned out first, they'll have to move. Somebody will probably want to change the name of the town to something fancier. This place as we know it will then be just a memory."

Hillary was about to make her remark when Nathan announced that it was time he was leaving. "If there's anything I can bring you, Aunt Begonia," he teased Aunt Fay, "or anything I can do, let me know. It's great to have you home from the hospital. I'll bet you'll be out jogging with the rest of us in no time."

The old woman chuckled, her dark head bobbing. "You have enough to do, son. Anyhow, I have to admit that my grandniece, Hillary here, is taking good care of me. We took it for granted that she was nothing but a spoiled city brat when she came here. But she's surprising us. Wait," she called when Nathan was as far as the door leading into the inn. "There is something you can do for me. When you have some extra time and need to earn some cash, you can give Ed Tandy a hand cleaning out the tool shed and barn."

Nathan grinned. "I'll find time to help him, Aunt Begonia."

Hillary jumped up before Nathan could disappear, intending to walk with him as far as the lobby. She'd like to talk about something not so heavy as the evening's conversation. And get better acquainted. But as she caught up with him, he moved away, muttering, "See you." He bolted off as if she were poison.

For a while Hillary stood there, puzzled and about half mad. Where was he coming from, anyway? He made her feel as if she had ten dozen warts on her face. Why wouldn't he give her a chance? A pox on him, then! Why waste her time even thinking about Nathan Webb when plenty of gorgeous guys in town were eager to date her? She'd never get anywhere with him, so she might as well let him go. Dumb thought. He'd never been hers in the first place.

She wandered back to the deck, filled with a turmoil of emotion. Until Aunt Fay spoke, she'd forgotten she was still out there. "So what do you think of my young friend, now? Sure wish I could read your mind this minute, Hilly."

"I was thinking that Nathan doesn't like me for some reason," she answered, her face blazing. "It's hopeless." She dropped back into her chair dejectedly.

"Oh, I think you're wrong, there, Hillary." Her great-aunt made a sound that might have been a laugh.

Hillary looked at her, feeling like a frustrated child.

"You know, Hilly, Nathan may not like the competition. He's no idiot. He sees you going out with all these other boys, and he probably doesn't think he has a chance."

Was that it? Hillary was stunned, thinking it over. "Do you really think that's the problem? But, Aunt Fay, Nathan acts as if he doesn't even see me. Won't talk to me. If he'd ask me out, I'd go in a minute."

This time, Aunt Fay did laugh. "Give Nathan time. He's out of doors so much, he may be a little skittish around girls. I'd guess he's plenty aware of you. But he doesn't want to admit it yet, even to himself. The boy has some pride, you know. He dreads the idea of you turning him down, which is what he suspects will happen. Given time, he'll come around. He can't ignore and bury his feelings forever. He'll have to do something about them, take a chance. Don't give up on him. Nathan's worth—"

Hillary broke in, laughing, "Aunt Fay, I think you

have a crush on him, yourself!"

"Well, I do! You don't expect me to lie about it, do you? I tell you, if Nathan doesn't get a scholarship to college so he can be a geologist, and if his dad's business won't pay enough to send him, I intend to help out with his education myself. That's how fond I am of Nathan Webb. Of course, I think the world of Virginia and Charles, they're good friends; but that boy of theirs, he's special."

For some time after that, neither of them spoke. The moon began to climb in the night sky, and the first stars appeared. The air was cool and tingly with the smell of peppermint from the distilleries. Hillary felt languid, drowsy, but she didn't want to move to go inside to bed. She was surprised that Aunt Fay was still up this late, but she was getting a lot better.

"Aunt Fay?"

"Yes?"

"I've been thinking about something. The electronics plant and all it stands for is here, and it can't be stopped." Maybe to the benefit of everybody, but she knew Aunt Fay wasn't ready to hear it. "But that doesn't mean people have to turn loose of the past altogether, their heritage, I mean. History. We don't need to forget. Even though we do have to live in the present, there is no reason not to value and remember the best—and most beautiful—from the past."

"Umm. Reminds me of something I read once: 'To improve quality of life, humanity needs to know where it's been, where it is, and where it wants to be.' That what you mean?" Aunt Fay asked.

"Yes, that. And I was thinking of some fun thing to do. I'm not sure just what. Maybe a festival of some kind. Or a ball. That's it, a grand ball for—everybody, a reminder."

"I think you've let the success of Ada and Morley's autograph party go to your head." She laughed. "It was a coup!"

"I suppose so. But think of it, a turn of the century ball. We could have it here at Rainsong Inn. Clear out the furniture from the dining room." She sat up straighter, becoming more excited as ideas came. "Everyone could come wearing Victorian clothes. They'd have to scour some antique stores, or sew their costumes."

"A turn of the century ball," Aunt Fay repeated with feeling. "There are a lot of people in this town nostalgic for the good old days who would go for something like that. You're right. For one night, we could bring those times to life again, and the Burton-Sipes tribe wouldn't matter for beans."

"It would last longer than for one night, Aunt Fay, the mood. For days and weeks people would be thinking about the ball, getting ready, looking forward to it. And they'd remember after. The good old days would be on their minds a long time." It was a way to counteract all the bad feelings about the plant, she thought. And a kind of transition to get the town over the hump. For her, it was a chance to explore an artsy idea, too.

We could get the newspaper into the act," Aunt Fay was saying. "Maybe Joe Lancaster, the editor, will dig back in his files of old newspapers for interesting stories and rerun them. A regular column, say, of true anecdotes about Reesville people from times gone by."

"Does that mean it's all right with you? We can have the ball for sure? It will take a lot of work to put it together—"

"I think it's a humdinger of a plan. I've got friends, Hilly, and I've got a telephone. I'll get a committee started on it right away to help you, unless someone can show me why we shouldn't do it. Like I said, there's folks in town who'll be excited about this. They'll help. If my hips were completely well, I'd dance up a storm. But I do want to be there, anyhow."

"I wonder where I'll find a dress for me?" Hillary mused, dreaming. "I might have to have one made. Do you have any old books, Aunt Fay, that would show fashions from Victorian times? Something I could have copied?"

"I might have some books. But first you better take a look in the attic here at the inn. Don't know for sure what's up there. Maybe just some dusty rags. But I kind of remember some better dresses put away with mothballs and the like, to preserve them. When I married Mr. Renshaw, he showed me the whole place, even up there. He thought the dresses should be thrown out, but I told him they weren't taking up any needed space. To let them alone. They made me think of the grand ladies who wore them, and I didn't want those fair dames' ghosts haunting me because I destroyed what little earthly goods was left of them."

It sounded marvelous: the secret life of old clothes.

"Aunt Fay, don't you think it's time we went to bed?" she asked. She could hardly wait, now, for tomorrow. To go up into Rainsong Inn's attic. Before she turned-in, she dialed Lei's phone number from Aunt Fay's office and invited her to go attic-exploring with her the next day. Lei agreed, but Hillary wished Lei'd sounded even a fraction as excited as she felt.

Chapter Twelve

Off to the side of the stair landing on Hillary's floor was a door, and according to Aunt Fay, the door opened to stairs that led to the attic. A large third floor of the inn, not actually used. Right after breakfast the next morning, flashlights in hand, Hillary led Lei up the narrow, dust-coated steps to an enormous, cobwebby room.

"I don't know why I let you talk me into this," Lei said, her eyes big in the gloom. "What a junky old place."

"You do, too, know. You wanted to get out of helping your mother make raspberry jam this morning." Hillary made out a single bulb hanging from the ceiling at either end and was surprised when she pulled a chain and the first light flicked on. They could see a lot better. Looking around, she realized that it had probably been ages since anyone had prowled around up here.

It was wonderful! Piled in corners were stacks of old papers and magazines. "How I'd like to dig into those." She pointed at them. There were tattered cartons of unknown contents and endless stacks of old books. She saw several trunks, some flat-topped and some camel-back. Her throat dried with expectation, excitement.

But Lei exclaimed, "Ugh," as she traced a finger along the back of a ragged velvet chair.

"Your trouble is that your eye is trained to hit the basket with your basketball and not to appreciate beautiful old things like these," Hillary explained, teasing. "We've got to reform you, Lei." When she opened the first door of a pair of makeshift wardrobe closets, a musty odor filled the air.

"Sure," Lei got back at her, laughing, "I'll bet the mice think that stuff is super, too."

"No, I don't think they got in here, too tight or something. No varmints." But she half expected the garments inside to crumble when she touched them. They didn't. The fabrics seemed woven to last an eternity if necessary.

While Lei moseyed about, she counted three long skirts. They were silk, she thought. One black, one turquoise, the third brown. There were a lot of blouses. "I think in the old days blouses were called shirtwaists," she called informationally to Lei.

"Whoopee!" Lei's muffled retort came from a far dark corner where only her blonde head shone like a light.

Hillary laughed and continued to examine the shirt-waists. Most of them were white, decorated with tucks, embroidery, and lace. Sleeves, even on the striped calico everyday dresses that she found, were balloon fat at the shoulder and very narrow down from the elbow.

What a find! She combed through them. But she didn't see *her dress,* one she wanted to wear. It had to be perfect. Most of these clothes were for an older woman.

Like Aunt Fay, Mavina, or Virginia Webb. Aunt Fay would be able to outfit half the town for the ball, if she wanted.

"I wish Aunt Fay could see all this, but there's no way she can manage all those stairs, yet," she mumbled aloud. "Just wait until I tell her what's up here. It's like another time, another world, isn't it, Lei? Such treasure! Like that tall old record player you're looking at," she told her. "It should be where people can see and enjoy it. And that huge painting of the bald eagle, *ooh.* And the old wall telephone and the wicker rocking chair—they're wonderful." Aunt Fay probably had not been up into the attic since she married Stuart Renshaw and had forgotten most of what was up here.

"You really do get carried away, don't you?" Lei marveled, coming to join her.

"Yes, I guess I do." Looking again in the closet, Hillary took out several garments and handed them to Lei. Aunt Fay had to see these for herself. There was no doubt she could find a perfect costume. From the second closet, she chose a rose crepe gown, a black silk skirt with a matching jacket, and a silky plaid dress and draped them over her arm. The latter dress with its tucked pigeon breast and peplum waist was super old-fashioned.

"We're going to have a fashion show, you and me," she told Lei. "We'll need a safety pin here and there, because most of these things will be too big, but it will be fun to try them on and model for Aunt Fay."

Lei looked more cheerful. "Okay. That sounds like more fun than up here. I'm ready for the real world again."

They found Aunt Fay in the dining room with Mavina, having their mid-morning coffee. Clatter from the kitchen told that Howard was busy with breakfast dishes. Changing in the pantry, giggling and perspiring, Hillary and Lei struggled into one outfit after another. In friendly competition, holding their heads high as they had seen professional models do, they swept and swirled about the dining room. Aunt Fay and Mavina broke up with laughter when Hillary got caught in a fit of sneezing.

"The clothes will have to go to the cleaners." Aunt Fay wiped her eyes. "Somebody who'll know how to clean them without ruining them. I've spotted my outfit. How about you, Mavina? For the ball I've been telling you about?"

"I'm not much for dancing"—Mavina eyed the girls over her coffee cup—"but I'd like to get into one of those black bell skirts and one of the white lacy shirts. Do you suppose I could? There may be problems with my middle —I don't have a tiny wasp-waist you may have noticed."

"Oh, you can try, Mavina." Hillary twirled up to their table. She curtsied. "And now, mesdames, we're off to the attic again to look for underwear."

"Not me," Lei said quickly. "I think my mother said something about an early lunch. I really have to get out of these duds and get home. Okay?" She looked at Hillary with a regretful grin.

Hillary sighed. "Okay. You've suffered enough. Go ahead home and miss the fun." Exploring attics plainly wasn't Lei's bag. "Thanks for coming by."

❧

WHEN LEI HAD GONE, HILLARY HEADED AGAIN FOR THE attic stairway. Behind her, she heard Aunt Fay remark,

"My grandniece is a cutie, isn't she? I've come to count on her for so much this summer."

Mavina replied, "She sparks up the place for certain. If she wasn't here, it wouldn't be the same. I'd miss her."

A small glow of pleasure warmed Hillary, and she smiled to herself. They hadn't seen anything, yet! She could more than manage, she could shape her life and do things for other people in the bargain, she was beginning to realize. All summer long she had been aware of this feverish worry, desire, to know herself. To make good, to feel solid again, a real person. Lately, she had the feeling she was getting somewhere.

In the attic again, she pawed her way through one trunk after another, for undergarments and accessories. She made a pile of things by the top of the stair that she wanted to take down: bloomers—their outfits might as well be totally authentic—chemises, petticoats, all trimmed lavishly with lace. And as a joke for Mavina, a stiff-boned corset. She tossed two more corsets on the pile, realizing that they might be a necessity for everybody, herself included, if she could find a dress. These old-fashioned clothes were very small-waisted.

Thinking at first that it was a petticoat, only more gorgeous than the rest, she found the dress at last. She drew the white garment slowly from a trunk, her breath catching. She stood up and held it against her, her heart hammering as joy made her feel tingly all over. It was cotton, she thought, but woven so fine it felt like silk. From the high neck, the bodice was trimmed on either side by a gauzy ruffle, fuller over the leg-o-mutton sleeves. The small, nipped-in waist was banded in lace like the neckline. The full, bell-shaped skirt that flowed from the waist was trimmed with three wide lace bands.

Hillary peeled out of her shirt and jeans there in the attic, unexplainable tears springing to her eyes. Dizzy, breathless, she pulled the dress over her head, bringing it gently down into place. Snug, but it fit. Maybe it could be let out. She lifted the skirt to her cheek. Wonderful, beautiful dress. Who had worn it so long ago? Was it for something very special? Graduation, a summertime ball, a concert? The dress should be in a museum for thousands to see, but first she would wear it to the turn of the century ball. If Aunt Fay okayed it. Sure, she would. The dress didn't belong up here, unseen, unappreciated.

She was glad Lei couldn't see her. She wouldn't understand in a million years. Hillary wiped her eyes, a new thought coming to her. She wouldn't want to go to the ball alone; she wanted a handsome escort. But who? Which of the gorgeous guys would be perfect for her, for the fabulous evening it was going to be? She scratched her head anxiously, wondering.

～

AFTER HER MORNING SPENT IN THE ATTIC, FEW MALES under age thirty escaped Hillary's consideration as a possible escort candidate as they came into the gift shop, ate in the dining room, or as she ran into them on the streets of Reesville. She would not wait for someone to ask her, she decided. If she could settle on a guy she felt was right, she would do the asking.

She thought of Tony Redstone, tall, older, with his wonderful dry sense of humor. When she'd started a new datebook, the first being filled, Tony was the first entry. They had gone to an All-Indian Rodeo, an event very big with some Oregonians it seemed. Tony was nice, a lot of fun, but she made up her mind that rodeo would never make her list of favorite entertainments. She thought it was ridiculous for animals and cowboys to slam one another around all over the place.

There was Dave Bellah and Stratton, but neither possibility brought any enthusiasm. Cary Blake was out, so were most of the others she could think of, fun guys though they were. She considered Nathan Webb with a discouraged feeling, ready to cry. What if he turned *her* down? Aunt Fay claimed he liked her, but she must be wrong. Nathan probably felt she just wasn't his type, or something. Anyway, her chances with him looked—*blah.*

OTHER THAN HER NOT HAVING A DATE FOR IT, BALL preparations moved ahead rapidly. The entire town seemed to be involved, with Aunt Fay turning out to be a surprisingly efficient co-chairman for the event. It was set for the end of August, a farewell-to-summer, farewell-to-Reesville-as-it-was, gala. She could hardly wait.

Hillary did her share and more, helping to repaint the huge dining room, which they closed for a weekend. She washed windows and helped hang new draperies. Abby Ross, close-mouthed, usually worked alongside her. But Abby shared no interest in the coming ball. Once in a while she disappeared, leaving Hillary to work alone, which she didn't mind. She relaxed, smiled, and could even sing if she felt like it. Things hard to do in Abby's glum presence.

It wasn't easy to explain even to herself, but she had a kind of fear that Abby's unhappiness might be contagious. She would catch the disease, and it would bring to the surface her own pain, caused by the separation from her parents. She didn't want to be like Abby, swallowed up in her own misery and feeling nothing else. Abby was like a stereo needle, stuck in a groove, unable to accept change and go on. So Hillary stayed away from her as much as she could. At the same time, she didn't want to be unkind to Abby.

When Abby would show up after a disappearance, she would be red-eyed and morose. Feeling guilty and sorry for her, Hillary made a few tries to help her, going so far as to suggest, once, that Abby see a doctor. Abby managed a smile, and then laughed at her. So Hillary didn't know what to do except give up. Abby's private life could stay her own affair if that's how she wanted it. Maybe she could make up to her children what she couldn't feel for their mother. She didn't want to think of Abby as a self-pitying pain, but it was just hard not to.

One afternoon as she was about to duck out of the dining room at the same time Abby entered, Hillary changed her mind and came back. "Abby, I have an idea," she began helpfully. "I'd like to take over some of your chores so you can spend more time with your kids and your mother, more time at home." Maybe she had been wrong to play with the kids so much, taking them from Abby. Being with her own children more would probably be good medicine for Abby, she thought.

She was shocked so see that Abby looked threatened and was angry. "I-I can't work part-time," Abby sputtered. "I wouldn't earn enough. Don't take my job!" Tears welled in her eyes.

Hillary felt instantly ashamed. "Look, Abby, I didn't mean—I would cover for you, that's all. I wouldn't be paid, it would be the same as if you were working." She reached out to touch Abby's arm, but Abby drew back.

"Hilly, maybe you mean to be nice, but I'd like for you to mind your own business. And leave me alone! Please."

There it was, she couldn't win. It wasn't worth arguing about. She might have felt hurt, but as it was she felt relief, as though she'd been suddenly freed. Abby could do her thing, and she'd do hers, then.

OUTSIDE THESE DAYS, AT ODD HOURS OFF FROM HIS usual job, Nathan helped Ed Tandy, though it had nothing to do with preparations for the ball. He was helping Ed reroof the carriage house. She looked forward to seeing Nathan's lean, blue-jeaned form down in the inn's backyard when he came to assist Ed. Often, she was too busy for more than a glimpse, but even that was enough to set her heart stupidly racing. With feelings that made her wonder.

The day Mavina baked cinnamon rolls, she set aside the merchandise she was unpacking, locked the door of the gift shop, and took a plate of rolls out to where Ed and Nathan worked. Nathan was on the carriage house roof, Ed directing him from below.

"Time for a break," she called gaily, her skirts swishing as she crossed the grass to them. "I brought you a present."

"I'm sorry, honey," Ed apologized, looking them over, "but I can't eat yummies like that. Doctor's orders. Have to take care of the old heart. Can't have too much sugar. They sure look good, though."

"I'm sorry I tempted you, then," Hillary said. "Nathan, how about you?"

He dropped down off the roof and came to take a cinnamon roll. Then he moved a few steps away. As though there was a circle drawn around her, marked "forbidden territory!" If the line was visible, she'd kick it to pieces and make him cross over! Instead, she pretended not to care, turning to Ed. "So you're going to escort Aunt Fay to the ball? Are you going to do it up right, bring her flowers and everything?" she teased.

Ed reared back, and his eyes sparkled. "For my gal, nothing is too good. I may pick every flower on this place and have them trucked around to the front door. What do you think?"

"Tied with a million miles of ribbon, I can't think of anything more romantic." Hillary laughed with him. "Aunt Fay would love it." She watched Nathan from the corner of her eye. He smiled quietly to himself at their joking, but he said nothing. Just stood there, looking every inch a handsome hunk. She offered him a second cinnamon roll, which he took with a soft, "thanks," she almost couldn't hear. She talked and joked with Ed for several minutes longer. Nathan went to sit on the ground, his back against the carriage shed, eating his cinnamon roll as if nothing else in the world was of any importance. To him, probably nothing was!

She wanted to scream at him. But she kept her emotions in check as she told the two of them, "I have to go in. I left the shop with nobody to watch it. I may have customers waiting for me to reopen. Bye."

Back inside the gift shop, she fumed. Nathan Webb wasn't worth a thought. He was a retard. All he knew was small town politics, ruined riverbanks, and crud like that. And if he never noticed her, she couldn't care less.

It was an hour or two later, and she was alone in the shop, when she thought she heard a noise. She looked up to see Nathan standing just inside the glass door. She stared at him, then she wordlessly went back to work wrapping a gift for a telephone customer. Forced into it, he might find his tongue and say something first, for a change. She was not about to speak to him.

A few minutes passed. Nathan prowled quietly around inside the shop while she covertly watched. She got the Scotch tape she was using wound about her finger instead of on the package where she wanted it, and she fought to get herself free. Why didn't he just go away? She freed her finger and started again. She tried to ignore the feelings of elation, happiness, stirring inside her simply because *he* was in the shop. It was useless to feel this way. She glanced up and saw Nathan turning to go. "Can I help you?" she almost shrieked. "Were you looking for something special?" What nerve he had, to try to leave without saying so much as "hi" or "goodbye"?

He turned back, his clear blue eyes meeting hers. "Yeah."

"What?"

"A book. I've run out of things to read."

He liked to read, then. And he would talk to her if he had to. They were getting somewhere. Her heart flip-flopped. "What do you like to read? Westerns? Science fiction? Suspense?" she asked in a high voice.

"Biography. I just finished Theodore Roosevelt. Pretty good. Thought I'd find something else like it in here. But I don't see anything." He nodded toward her bookshelf, and he swallowed so hard she saw his Adam's apple bob in his tan throat.

Hillary sighed. "Hey, I think you're right. We don't have any biographies. We don't have room to stock many good books. How about this new Clive Cussler novel?" She went to the bookshelves and moved a stack of *Bats in the Basement, Ants in the Attic,* that were in the way on the floor. She came back with the novel. "Look it over," she offered.

She watched his profile as he examined the inside of the jacket flaps front and back. She could swear he wasn't actually reading any of it. "I'll take it," he said. He fished in his jeans' pocket for the money, gave her a twenty-dollar bill and thrummed his fingertips on the edge of the counter while she got the change. "Will you go on a picnic with me Sunday?"

The invitation came so suddenly, and it was so unexpected, Hillary's hand dropped into his as she was counting out his change. Money spewed onto the counter. "I'm sorry," she cried, snatching up the coins and bills and cramming them into his palm. She wondered if she'd heard him right. Had he asked her to go on a picnic? Was it a—a date? She didn't know people went on picnics anymore. She was still trying to get over her amazement, to say something, when he mumbled, sounding disappointed, "It's okay if you're going to be busy with somebody else."

"But I'm not." Didn't he know that if he really wanted to take a girl out he shouldn't give up so easy? "I'd love to go on a picnic with you," she assured him. "I haven't been on a picnic in years; it'll be fun. And let me bring the food. I won't have to fix it, Mavina will, and she's the best."

He stared at her as if her answer was totally opposite to what he was ready for. "You're sure? If you are—well, okay then! Let's say we leave here around—what time?"

"Twelve?"

"Twelve it is. Great. I'll come by for you."

From then until Sunday, Hillary lived in an unmanageable state of ecstasy, coupled with anticipation, curiosity, and concern. She was going on a picnic with Nathan! Finally. She just knew, too, that a date with Nathan was going to be different. She hoped whatever happened, that she would do the right thing. He had to like her.

Chapter Thirteen

On Sunday, Nathan and Hillary drove out of town in his yellow pickup truck. Her arm nervously encircled Aunt Fay's wicker picnic basket on the seat next to her. In a half hour or so, Nathan drew the pickup over to the side of the road and stopped.

"Something tells me we're going to climb that mountain," Hillary said, peering out the window. "It's beautiful." The slope was dotted with small blue and white flowers amid rocky outcroppings and yellow bushes.

"It's a hill, not a mountain."

"So what do I know? I'm from Iowa where most of the land is as flat as your hand. Still looks like a mountain to me." She liked being here next to Nathan so much, she waited before getting out of the pickup.

"Actually, it's a butte."

"Hey, Nathan, are we going to argue about this?" she joked. Then she saw his face. He was flushing crimson, and she realized he had taken her literally. Instantly, she was sorry. How was he to know she was just kidding? "I was making a joke. Dumb joke. I'm glad you brought me here, Nathan. To this hill—butte—mountain, whatever it is. Let's go climb it. Mavina's fixed a fantastic lunch, and it deserves to be earned."

He studied her face for a moment. Those blue eyes were not the lying kind, she felt. She'd been wrong about Nathan not liking her. Very wrong. Her face warmed under his gaze.

In a moment, Nathan seemed to come to, looking embarrassed. He jumped from the pickup and came around to open her door, taking the picnic basket from her. "Let's go."

HALFWAY UP THE BUTTE, THEY STOPPED TO REST ON A rocky ledge. "This dirt pile feels like a mountain," Hillary panted, "a big mountain. Maybe we should eat here, not go any further."

He laughed. "C'mon, we can make it to the top. I want you to see the view. And like you said, Mavina's food should be earned." With a pretended casualness, he caught her hand and pulled her up. "Let's go."

Along the way he stopped now and then to name a wildflower or a tree, when she asked. And other times when she didn't. He allowed her to pick a bouquet of Queen Anne's lace, telling her it was common wild carrot. But pretty, he agreed. When they came to a blue flower she wanted to pick, he asked her to leave it. "It's a Hall's aster," he told her. "It's rare, and in another few years it may become extinct. We can help by leaving it here to go to seed."

"Well, if there's anything I don't want to be, it's a wildflower killer." She saw his embarrassment and quickly added, "I'm kidding again. Look, Nathan, I'm interested. I like flowers and rocks and things like that the same as you do. I just don't know as much about them. You can teach me."

"Are you sure? I'm not apologizing for what I am, but—I don't want anybody, especially you, thinking I'm an oddball, either." He shrugged thoughtfully, dropped to a squat, and motioned her down beside him. She flopped to the ground and caught a dry piece of grass to nibble on. She guessed that he wanted to explain more about himself, and she was just glad he felt he could talk to her.

"It must seem silly for a guy to know about flowers," he said quietly. "But to me they are just one part of the whole—that's being destroyed. As far as I'm concerned, disappearing plants, like the wild, three-colored monkeyflower and the yellow lady's slipper and the golden paintbrush, are signs of abuse. Much of the natural world is in danger. I don't know if I'm saying this right—"

She nodded for him to go on.

"We still have too many forest fires caused by campers, for one thing," he told her, staring into the distance with a frown. "We've built highways into what should have been left alone as wilderness. For people, of course. The heavy recreational use of lands, the development of homes and towns and cities is doing away with the land that was. The beauty everybody supposedly appreciates and wants preserved. I don't have all the answers, but someday I'll have some of them. Maybe it's crazy to worry about things like that. Balance. But—I do."

"I'm glad, and I don't think it's crazy at all. I'm sure

too many people, like me, don't stop to think enough about such things."

"You're okay." He grinned and stood up. "Now for the view. Except for a little pollution, it's still there. Onward and upward."

More comfortably this time, he took her hand, and she was aware of how much she liked the feeling of hers inside his. Nathan was all right, too. The sun poured down, warm, and in the dry grasses, small nameless insects hummed. At the top of the butte, they took seats Indian fashion on a fallen, waist-high log, viewing the world below. He pointed out Reesville, a miniature toy town centering an area of lush farmland.

"It's truly beautiful." Hillary sighed. "Refreshing. It makes a person feel good, just to look. Thanks, Nathan." A while later, she opened the picnic basket. "Are you ready for this? We have chicken dagwoods, melon, oatmeal cookies, and fruit juice."

"I think I am. But what's a chicken dagwood?" Cautiously he accepted the large sandwich, which threatened to fall to pieces.

"You'll like it. A chicken dagwood is lettuce, slices of chicken, bacon, dollops of sour cream, blue cheese, avocado—"

"Whoa!"

"But that's not all. There is also sliced tomato, sliced boiled egg, and oh, yes, whole-grain bread." They laughed. "It's one of my favorites," she told him.

"Hurry and eat your sandwich or I get all the oatmeal cookies."

They ate quietly, taking a moment now and then from looking at each other to view the scene spread below them. "It's killing me to admit it," Hillary finally told him, wiping her mouth, "but I think there is a possibility that Oregon is more beautiful than Iowa."

"You know it is. And this is only a small part of Oregon. What about the ocean, has anyone taken you to see the great Pacific Ocean yet?"

She shook her head.

"You're kidding! All the guys in this town rushing you, and none of them has taken you to the beach? Midwesterners usually go bananas over it, too. Tell you what, let's pretend the Pacific is my ocean, and nobody gets to show it to you but me, all right?"

"I see nothing wrong with that. After all, it is your ocean. Do you have any other mountains you'd like to show me? Besides this—butte?"

"Oh, do I! Not just the Cascades, but the Blue Mountains, and the Steens. In the far northeast corner of this state there are the Wallowas, known as the Alps of Oregon. They're fantastic."

"That, I would like to see. I loved a book that belonged to my mother, called *Heidi*. The story is set in the Swiss Alps. It always made me hungry for bread and cheese; the girl and her grandfather were always eating bread and cheese." At Nathan's puzzled look, she laughed. "You'd have to read it." She rummaged through the basket, rustling wads of plastic wrap. "No more cookies? Ah, one more. I'll share."

She broke the cookie in two and passed a half to Nathan. As he took it, their fingers brushed and her glance sprang to his, finding him looking at her as if he wanted to say something. "What?" she asked.

"M-m—Nothing. We better go on. There's a surprise down the other side. Something I want to show you."

The surprise was an old, abandoned one-room

schoolhouse, silvery gray, about the same size as the toolshed at Rainsong Inn. "I love it!" Hillary cried. "Why didn't I remember to bring my sketchbook? Now I'll have to draw it from memory." There were two small outhouses in back, labeled boy and girl, and in front, a flagpole without a flag. At one side was a rusty pump, and near it, empty swings moved ghostlike in the breeze. "It's adorable."

"My grandmother, my mother's mother, taught school here," Nathan told her. "She rode a white pony called Popcorn five miles every day to school to teach. Her largest attendance was something like twelve kids."

"I'll do a sketch for you. And if you can find a photograph I can copy, I'll draw in your grandmother on her pony, Popcorn, too."

He grinned down at her. "That'd be great."

They went into the schoolhouse, Nathan pushing open the door with care. "I wonder what it was like to go to school here in the olden days?" Hillary whispered, close behind him. "No cafeteria, no visual aids, no gymnasium—"

"It might have been fun. Grandmother said they sometimes went outside and held school sitting in the grass under a tree on warm spring days. Another time, one winter, an owl built a nest in the chimney, which made the smoke from the pot-bellied stove back up into the schoolroom. Probably that one." He pointed. "It caused some excitement, she said."

Hillary laughed. "I don't think that could have happened at Abbott Elementary where I went to school. Very modern. We had at least a thousand kids. Needless to say, I didn't get to know hardly any of them well."

They went back outside, still walking lightly as

though to disturb the little school unnecessarily would be a grave wrong.

She ran to the swing and sat on the board seat. "Push me, please?"

He came, his muscled arms close as he caught the chain on either side of her. "Here you go." He took several steps back, holding her high in the air before he let go of the swing. They both laughed as she sailed forward.

For several minutes he pushed her in the swing. Each time she came back to his waiting arms, his hands, she felt his breath near her ear, and she could smell his fresh, ferny cologne. After a while, she touched her feet to the ground, stopping the swing. "Your turn," she said hollowly. What was happening to her, anyway? She felt weak, foolishly ill. Maybe it was the chicken dagwood sandwich. Or maybe it was…she got out of the swing and turned to go around it. She faced Nathan, looking into his eyes. His glance clung to hers, and she saw a reflection of her own feelings there. "Nathan—?"

Wordlessly he put his hands on her shoulders and drew her close. His lips met hers softly, briefly. They pulled away from one another then and stood staring into each other's eyes in a kind of disbelief. "What's going on, what is this with us?" she whispered.

Nathan kissed her long and lingeringly, as though to find out. "I knew this would happen," he said huskily, "if I ever got close to you. Hilly, I don't know how you feel about me, but I like you. More than *like*, I think. I can't believe you're here with me. I've dreamed about this, but I never thought it would happen. You're so pretty, beautiful. There's so many guys around town who—"

She put a finger to his lips. "There are mega guys

around town, yes, but I have to tell you the truth, Nathan. I've been in Oregon for more than two months. I've dated lots. But today has been the most wonderful time of my life. Honest."

He shook his head. "But—just a picnic?"

"I know, just a picnic. And you showed me Queen Anne's lace, explained Hall's asters to me, and the rest. We explored this old school, played on the swing." She was thoughtful a moment. "There was a time I might not have felt the way I do today," she went on. "I've come to appreciate *real* things, *real* people, this summer, not just the fancy and phony." She'd changed, although she didn't say so aloud. In Iowa, her life had been fun and easy, but not really enriching. Maybe that was part of why she looked so hard for the right boy to love. As good as her life had been, it hadn't been enough.

They climbed the hill again and started down the opposite side, stopping once to rest on a pile of rock. With a stick, Nathan curiously jabbed at small bits of stone. He took several specimens for more study at home.

"You know," Hillary told him lazily, "I do feel like Heidi, up here on this moun—butte."

"Except for the chicken dagwoods?"

"Except for the chicken dagwoods. We eat cheese and dark, thick bread. I'm Heidi, and you are Peter the goat boy."

"Where are my goats?"

"Oh, please, don't be so technical," she scolded, tossing a handful of grass at him. "They're asleep under some trees somewhere."

"Was Peter Heidi's boyfriend?"

"She married him."

"Whoops, walked into that one." He caught her hand

and pulled her to her feet. They kissed lightly, then they walked down the rest of the way to the waiting yellow pickup at the roadside.

"Can I see you again—go out, I mean?" Nathan asked her. He looked so scared and at the same time doubtful, she wanted to grab his cheeks and kiss him as she might a worried child.

"Of course." She leaned against the sun-warmed pickup door, smiling faintly at him. "Nathan, I've wanted you to ask me out for just about forever. Why didn't you, before now?"

A slow flush crept up his throat into his face. His eyebrows arched, came down, arched again as he hesitated. He shuffled in a tight circle in the roadway, his hands in his pockets, before looking at her. "I'm not sure I should tell you."

"I asked."

"Yeah, but this may get me into trouble, and I don't want that." He shrugged, beginning slowly, "From the first minute I saw you, in the back seat of Mrs. Renshaw's car, the day you came to town, I felt like you were somebody special. The kind of girl I wouldn't get many chances to meet. I was *zapped* from the start. Although I didn't want to be, because of all the other guys hanging around you. Tough competition, some great guys. I thought you'd just turn me down, anyway, and my ego would be gonged. Then, later, I got the idea that you might be the kind of girl who just wants to play games with guys, and I'm not into that. Now, I know diff—" Seeing her face, his voice died.

Games? He thought she played *games*? Her intentions to find the perfect boy this summer wasn't like that at all. She'd been as serious about wanting to find the right guy for her as she'd ever been about anything. Maybe more serious. She'd had fun, going out, but that was hardly a crime.

It hurt, it made her feel ill, that Nathan, *Nathan,* would see her as a light, empty-headed flirt, nothing more. Oh, god. She looked away from him, drew her arm away when she felt his touch. "You have me wrong, Nathan. But it doesn't matter. Forget it. I don't want to talk, anymore, and you don't have to see me."

He caught her hand tightly in his in spite of her resistance. "I think that would be just about impossible now, don't you? I really am sorry. I shouldn't have said anything. Forgive me. Look," he persisted, "I'm not perfect. I wish I knew as much about girls as I know about trees."

He sounded so cute, saying it, she had to smile through the threat of tears. "You mean that, don't you?"

"Yes. Please say you forgive me?"

"You're forgiven. Because, Nathan, I can't give you up, either." She walked into his waiting arms and laid her head on his shoulder. "And you are perfect, Nathan. Except for the one, teeny, tiny flaw. I'll teach you, so you'll know as much about girls as you know about trees. But let's pretend I'm the only girl, the only one who can teach you, okay?"

"You are the only girl."

AFTER THAT, WHEN HE HAD THE CHANCE, NATHAN WOULD bring his lunch and join her at the inn. They ate together at one of the picnic tables down by the river or sat talking on the grassy bank. She egged him on, loving to hear him discuss the things he knew about. On one occasion, Nathan pointed out an alder tree that worried him. Leafy and green, it leaned outward, hanging over the water. He explained that much of the earth around its roots had been washed away and that the tree itself would probably be lost in another flood.

"That's terrible," Hillary said. "It shouldn't die. It clings so stubbornly, so beautifully, to life there. Can't something be done to save it?"

"A revetment would help. Something to bolster it."

"Can't you get your father, the city council to see about one?"

"If I could get their attention, I'd try. Right now, they're involved with Burton-Sipes up to their eyeballs. Like whether or not BS"—he winked at her—"can just bump old residents off the land the company has bought."

SOMETIMES, SHE AND NATHAN WADED IN THE RIFFLES BY the water's edge. Once, they took the Ross children to picnic and wade with them. But it was quickly evident that both of them were uneasy, afraid of water. They pulled back, unable to enjoy it.

Nathan led them from the water and sat them down on the ground, then he squeezed in between them. "Got to tell you guys something, like a story. Listen to the water. The river is talking to you, hear the soft chuckles? It likes you. Of course, Old Man River doesn't want you to come out where it's too deep. He wants you to stay where it's safe, by the edge, with us, until you get to be good swimmers someday."

Hillary joined them on the ground, seated by Kirstie.

Keegan's voice was still husky from worry as he said, "My friend, Joey, has a wading pool. I like that better."

His little sister bobbed her blonde head, and she snickered behind her hands. "We can sit in it hard and make the water splash out."

Hillary hugged her, laughing. "I don't think we can do that with Mr. River, there's too much water in him."

"Old Man River, not Mr.," Nathan corrected with a grin. "It's all right, guys, to be cautious about Old Man River. But you can love and respect him, too. Know why? Because he's just as much a wonderful creation as we are. The river is a home for the fish that are Oregon's pride—trout, steelhead, and salmon, too, when the salmon are migrating to spawn. Would you like to go fishing for trout someday?" he asked them. They nodded eagerly.

"I'd like to go, too," Hillary said. "Can we take a boat?"

"We'll take a boat, because that's something else the river is good for, boating. Do you guys like to eat strawberries and green beans and have jack-o-lanterns for Halloween? Well, the river gives the farmer the water to irrigate his crops, too."

"You're funny." Hillary laughed out loud, looking at Nathan. "But so good with them. I'm glad that you like kids, too."

"Why pass up an opportunity to fill their little heads with some good propaganda? They listen. Older kids would think I was an airhead and go right on filling the river with their beer cans."

Later, they delivered the children over to Abby's mother who came wandering to the inn. And then, Nathan and Hillary stood on the inn porch, holding hands, saying goodbye. She blurted, "Nathan, will you be my escort to the turn of the century ball?" He had heard about it, now she went on to tell him the reasons behind the ball, and how much fun it would be.

"I'm sorry, Hilly." His face was red, and he looked miserable. "But I can't take you to the dance. You've been looking forward to it, and I'd only spoil everything. I'm not a good dancer."

"Let me teach you. You've certainly been teaching me about things—wildflowers, trees, the river. *Oregon*. It'll be a tradeoff."

With his thumb, he massaged the knuckles of her left hand one by one. "I don't like to think about it, but this one time I think you should go with some other guy, someone who can dance, a real expert. I can tell this is a special thing for you, and I don't want to ruin your good time."

"Nathan, I don't think I could have a bad time with you."

"No." He shook his head. "No."

The depth of her disappointment shocked Hillary, but she managed to tell him, "I don't want you to be miserable just to please me. If you really don't want to go, it's okay. But I can't help wishing…"

Maybe she could still get one of the gorgeous guys to go with her, one of the Burton-Sipes crew. But they held small appeal compared to Nathan. Just possibly, she had gotten a bit off track this summer, going out so often, with so many different guys. Her social life was like a blur when she thought about it. And not much fun anymore. Maybe she'd had too much of a good thing. Like the time when she was little and alone in the kitchen, and she had literally overdosed on half a chocolate cake. She couldn't look at dessert for some time after.

She honestly wished now that she could have a relationship with one neat guy, whom she could get to know really well. Preferably, Nathan. She thought he wanted that, too. After the dance, maybe then.

that *couldn't* happen.

Ironically, when he could—she could, just, it's painful to part. giving over, she could get to know. she was . . . Unfortunately, Nathan she thought he watched her from ... After the meal, they drove past

Chapter Fourteen

Posters, newspaper ads, and stories successfully spread the word about the turn of the century ball. Some of the more sophisticated Burton-Sipes people, and a few others, might not know or care, Hillary thought, but most of Reesville's residents were talking excitedly of little else. But time was running out, and she still didn't have an escort lined up.

When she counted and realized that she had turned down three, or was it five? invitations, Hillary wondered if she wasn't being too particular. Even Tony Redstone, gorgeous though he was, didn't seem to measure up anymore. Or Jimmy Field. Or—none of them. Nathan wasn't the only boy in the world. It only seemed that way, right? If these really were Victorian times, she would have to stay home alone for lack of a proper gentleman escort, having blown all her chances.

She worried about it as she brought down most of the clothing from the attic, outfitting any and all in need. Aunt Fay's rose silk crepe dress was ready and waiting. The dress she had chosen was clean and her outfit complete. Besides the beautiful white dress, she'd found a pair of soft white kid pumps with a grosgrain ribbon over the instep at the Homesteaders' Museum. Luckily, they fit, and the museum owner had agreed to lend them. Yet for her, the ball could still be a disappointment. Girl with perfect dress, girl with perfect shoes, girl with no guy.

Even so, when Stratton Smith came by the gift shop and mentioned the ball, and she guessed that he intended to ask her to go with him, she steered the conversation to Lei Haffner. Without his catching on to what she was up to, Hillary hoped, she finally convinced Stratt that Lei was the girl for him.

Which once again left her without a date for the ball. Why couldn't she be happy with any of them who asked? She was killing her own chances, but it was as though she just couldn't help it.

It was almost the countdown hour when she ran into Ryun Gillson as she was leaving Papa Juan's Tacos one evening alone, just finishing a junk-food snack—which she craved sometimes, in spite of Mavina's great cooking.

"I've been looking for you," Ryun said, smiling, "to tell you that I'll pick you up around seven-thirty."

"Pick me up?" She gave him a blank stare. "For what?"

"You forgot, didn't you?" he asked in amazement. "The barbecue down by the river with a bunch of the guys. You promised you'd go with me." His eyes, studying her face, showed a mixture of puzzled disappointment and hope. "It's tomorrow night!"

"Oh! Oh," she said. "No, I didn't forget." But she had. Until now. Did he tell her about the barbecue last week, or two weeks ago? Ryun was in the shop a lot. It was unbelievable that the date, or Ryun for that matter, could slip her mind. But going out so much, maybe she was due to get dates mixed up. Now, she wished she could get out of this one. The barbecue didn't sound like nearly so much fun as it had when he had asked her.

"Look," he said, as though reading her mind, "please don't back out on me. It's too late now for me to find another girl. Every available girl has been asked. There aren't enough girls to go around as it is. Please, Hillary?"

A promise was a promise. Trying to squelch her feeling of regret, she said, "I'm looking forward to it." She smiled. "I'll be ready, Ryun."

His warm smile of relief almost made keeping her commitment to him worth it. Ryun Gillson wasn't handsome in the usual sense, but he was unquestionably attractive in other ways. Waiting on him in the shop, she had found him amiable and fun to talk to.

Now he smoothed his short, crisp brown hair and grinned, his green eyes picking up his good humor in a sparkle. "Sure. I should have known you wouldn't miss the big bash. See you tomorrow night."

She waggled her fingers in farewell and hurried off toward the inn, sighing. She wasn't crazy about the prospect of going out with Ryun, with anybody right now. Except Nathan. But Nathan didn't want to take her to the ball and—maybe Ryun would.

〜

HILLARY REMEMBERED THAT ED HAD TOLD HER THERE was an encampment for Burton-Sipes workers down by the river, in a park southeast of town. She hadn't seen it, though, until she arrived with Ryun. She was reminded of a circus, or a carnival. There were lines of tents, campers, and motorhomes. Music blared from car stereos with doors flung open. There were guys and girls everywhere, a few of them attempting to dance on the hardpacked ground. It looked like fun.

"Gillson! Get over here," someone shouted from the direction of a black, late model pick up where the tailgate served as a bar. "What're you drinkin'?"

Ryun guided her toward the makeshift bar. She looked over the array of bottles, the two large beer kegs, and then she saw the carton of soda in back. "Seven-Up." She smiled in response to Ryun's questioning look.

"Give her a beer," Ryun said, grinning at the sweating, heavy-set young guy serving as a bartender. "And make mine a big one. We're going to get it on, tonight!"

"Just Seven-Up for me, please," she repeated. She didn't feel obligated to say that she was underage and that being sober didn't get in the way of her having a good time. She really didn't want a beer, anyway, and she did want 7-Up.

Ryun sighed, shaking his head. "Okay, for God's sake. Give her a Seven-Up."

With drinks in hand, they moved from group to group, and Ryun introduced her to some of the people she didn't know. Many of the girls she met were not from Reesville, since it was so small, but were from Lebanon, Albany, and other surrounding towns. For a while they joined a singing group, sitting on the riverbank. They listened to stories and jokes. But later, walking around, they came to a group discussing the Portland Blazers basketball team's prospects to win the NBA, and Hillary moved on when Ryun stopped to listen.

She made her way to a picnic area where hamburgers sizzled on a slew of outdoor grills set up for the occasion. Even the air smelled delicious. Tony Redstone was one of the cooks, and she asked, "How is everything, Tony?"

He looked up from his squatting position and mopped his forehead. "They make big chief work like common squaw," he complained with a mock frown. Then he added in his normal voice, "It's the only way I can make sure these babies get cooked until they're done. Some of these airheads would eat them raw and get trichinosis or some such, if you let them." Expertly, with a spatula, he flipped about a dozen patties over and clapped a bun on each. "How will you have your hamburger, my girl?" he asked Hillary.

"I like mine well done, too," she said with a laugh.

"Where'd you go?" Ryun's voice asked suddenly, behind her.

"Right here. Tony is a friend. He's making a special hamburger for me. How about one for you? Tony Redstone, this is Ryun Gillson." She pulled her hand away from Ryun's to accept the hamburger Tony passed to her.

"Next time, don't go running away." She didn't like the order, even though Ryun said it calmly, and he smiled.

Tony was smiling, too. "I wondered who the sap was who would bring a nice girl like Hillary to this brawl."

Although she wanted to laugh, she kept her face straight. Ryun seemed not to catch Tony's meaning, anyway. "Give her a plate," he ordered, "and put some of those beans on it." He pointed to the pot bubbling near Tony's arm. "Give her some potato chips, too. What are you doin', man? Take care of my girl."

"No beans, no chips." Hillary shook her head.

"With everything for me," Ryun continued to order Tony. He asked Hillary, "Are you sure? You want another hamburger, then. Fix her another one, Redstone."

Hillary counted silently to ten. Ryun was fast making her feel as if she ought to be wearing a collar and leash, with her plate labeled "Fido." The guy didn't own her. "Ryun," she said patiently, smiling up at him in the light from the fires, "I have a mind of my own. And I know to ask for something if I want it. I don't want another hamburger, I hardly ever eat more than one. I hate pork and beans, and greasy potato chips make me break out. All right?"

"I get it," he said with a groan, "you're one of those independent types. A women's-libber who has to do everything for herself."

"Far from it, I'm—" She broke off, feeling it was hopeless to explain to him, again. "Let's forget it, Ryun, all right? What else would you like to talk about? Tell me what you're going to do this fall, when your work with Burton-Sipes is finished. Or will you stay on with them in some job?"

She caught Tony's grin of sympathy, his amusement as she let Ryun propel her toward a pair of camp chairs. Evidently, he had Ryun sized up as a flake; funny she hadn't noticed it before. The guy was too possessive. He would be happier with a paper doll, a girl he could constantly maneuver. Live and learn. She could plead a headache and ask him to take her back to "Tara." But she should stick it out for a while. She had agreed to this date, no one else made her come. She was glad, though, that she was with Ryun only tonight. From his conversation, she gathered that he expected their relationship to continue. No way, of course. And she'd have to make that clear.

Much later, she was waiting by the car for Ryun, who had gone to his trailer for a jacket, when Cary Blake wandered out of a noisy crowd toward her. She had seen him around tonight, a few times, but they hadn't spoken.

"What's new?" he asked her now.

"I keep busy, Cary."

"That big dance coming up, how about going with me?"

She shook her head. "Thanks, anyway."

"I'm sorry about that night, Hillary."

"I'm sorry, too."

Cary kissed the tips of his fingers and blew the kiss to her, just in time for Ryun, returning, to see. "What's going on?" he asked suspiciously. "Back off, Blake. Hillary is my girl."

It was so ridiculous, Hillary shook her head and started to laugh as she climbed into the car. In a way, she was glad she'd come here tonight—because she had learned something definite from it. She wasn't Ryun's girlfriend, she was Nathan's. He was too special in her feelings for it to be otherwise. She'd stay home from the ball, or go alone, or whatever. Because she wouldn't enjoy it with anyone else.

SHE WAS DELIGHTED WHEN NATHAN CAME TO THE INN right after breakfast the next morning. Until she saw the look on his face. "Is nuclear war imminent, honey?" she teased. "You're not leaving town? Is somebody in your family sick or hurt? You've wrecked your pickup, then?"

"None of the above," he answered, swallowing in exaggeration as though he had been eating cactus. "I've decided to ask you to go to the dance with me. That is, if it isn't too late and nobody's beat me to it, will you?"

She looked at him, speechless. "Nathan, really?" she gasped, finding her voice. A flood of happiness warmed her all over. She threw her arms about his neck. "I've been asked, but it was impossible to say 'yes' to anyone else. Thank you, Nathan. But what made you change your mind?"

"Ed Tandy got after me. He was really burned with me when he heard that I turned you down. He said, 'In my day, no proper gentleman would refuse a lady.' Another thing, even worse, I haven't been able to sleep nights, picturing you going with some other guy. So Mom has been teaching me some dance steps she *thinks* might fit the music they'll play waltzes and stuff. She says that I'm pretty good. But I have to warn you, she suffers 'mother-blindness' when it comes to my faults."

"Oh, it's all right! As long as you're going to be with me, everything is going to be great." Virginia Webb wasn't blind. She was a very smart lady.

Nathan came back at noon, and they took their sandwiches down by the river to eat. Although her own world seemed close to perfect, she couldn't help but see that Nathan was worried. For some time she watched him, then she asked, "What else is bothering you, Nathan? You must be upset about something more than taking me to the ball."

"I'm not really concerned about the dance; I'm glad I'm going, now. It's something else, you're right." For a moment he was quiet, then he went on, "The problem is a little disagreement with my dad. I'm trying to get him to see something my way." He sighed heavily. "But he thinks I'm an idealistic kid. He won't take me seriously."

"About what?"

"Those people. The families being tossed out of their homes over on Whitman and Booth Streets." He looked agitated, angry, and at the same time, helpless.

Whitman Street had a familiar ring to Hillary, but she couldn't think who she might know who lived there. Lei, possibly. She waited for Nathan to go on.

"This particular piece of property was zoned for multiple family housing sometime back, although for years there have only been old, single-family houses on it. Rentals, mostly," he told her. "Burton-Sipes recently bought the land from an investor who lives in Portland, who doesn't really give a darn about any people. Burton-Sipes intends to tear the houses down and build some deluxe condominiums to house their executives. Dad says according to city law, Burton-Sipes has no responsibility toward the people being evicted. They don't have to find them new places to live. But I think they should be asked to do it."

"Well, Nathan, morally they ought to do it, but I can see your dad's point. A big company would probably balk at something that costly—relocating a bunch of people."

"But why not ask? Burton-Sipes may be able to afford it, and I can think of a good reason for them to do the decent thing. From now on, Burton-Sipes will be a part of this town. Maybe, if they funded this new housing, or at least helped, it would build some good will. Soften up some of the residents who are furious that they came here in the first place. I doubt that Burton-Sipes wants to be the big enemy forever."

Alarm struck Hillary suddenly. "Nathan! I just remembered who lives on Whitman Street. Abby Ross! They just can't throw her out; it would be the last straw. She already thinks life is against her. We have to do something!"

"Calm down, honey," he urged, clasping her arms. "I was about to explain. I went to the library to do some research, and I've talked to people, too. Sooner or later, those old houses on Whitman and Booth Streets will have to come down; some of them are hardly more than shacks. That stretch between the business district and the newer residential district is considered ideal for multiple family housing-apartments, duplexes, and so on, because it's close to businesses. But out on the northwest edge of town, there's some vacant land for sale." He hesitated.

"And—?" Hillary urged him to go on.

"I think Burton-Sipes could buy it, get the county-involved, and work with the public housing authorities to build some houses for low-income citizens. Burton-Sipes should donate the land and hire the contractors, the county should pay for the houses, and they would be county property to manage. It'd be a place for those poor people so they could stay here."

"It's a lot to ask." She shook her head. "But it's a great idea, Nathan. Do you think Burton-Sipes might do this? And"—she grinned at him—"do you think they'd listen to an idealistic kid like you?"

"Why not try? Several people are up in arms about those people being uprooted, but nobody has come up with a solution like this one that I know of."

"And," she said slowly, "why would Burton-Sipes offer to do anything at all until *somebody* says, 'Look, here's where you're wrong, and here is something you

can do to remedy it.' Can I help, Nathan? Write letters?
Stage a protest? What?"

"Right on!" Nathan nodded, looking pleased. "It's
great to have you with me. And I'll keep you informed. I
intend to keep badgering Dad about this; I think he
should be the go-between, though, not us.

"And I figure that until Burton-Sipes is approached,
no one can be sure what they'll say. I think Dad, as
mayor, and his council members, ought to call those guys
to account, though."

She was thoughtful a moment. "Nathan, I think I
finally know what small town politics is, at least partly.
It's trying to help the people who can't help themselves,
isn't it?" And if that's what it was, she did want to be a
part of it.

THE DAY OF THE BALL ARRIVED, AND HILLARY SET ASIDE
most of the afternoon to get ready. Even so, there was
hardly time enough. *How did Victorian girls ever get to
anything on time?* she wondered, frantically trying to coil
her hair and fasten it the way she wanted it, atop her
head. What good did it do to wear a one-hundred-year-
old dress if your hair looked like something from the
latest *Seventeen* magazine?

Determined, she worked until she had it right. It
mattered so much how she looked to Nathan tonight, she
wanted to be very pretty for him. Once, she wondered
what he might be wearing, but she knew it didn't matter.
That she would be with him was the only important
thing.

They had agreed to meet down in the lobby just

before eight. At five after, Hillary started down the stairs, short of breath. Below her, a crowd was gathering, chattering and moving about. Where was Nathan? Then she saw him near the door, close to a corner. He was dreamy, she thought, unbelievably perfect in an old-fashioned pearl gray tuxedo. His hair was neatly trimmed, and he held a pearl gray top hat in one hand. He was stunningly handsome, to tell the truth! "Nathan," she whispered softly to herself.

As she moved down the stairs, hurrying toward him, she knew that none of the gorgeous guys, the Burton-Sipes crew, would have suited the role of a Victorian gentleman half as well. Nathan, in his own way, was more gorgeous than any dozen of the others!

"You're beautiful," he said the minute they came together. His eyes were shining, his smile more confident than she had ever seen it.

"I was thinking the same thing. I mean, Nathan, you have no idea how good-looking you are!" She pulled him with her into the dining room, then into the hall and outside onto the deck, away from the noisy crowd. She wanted this moment alone with him before the dancing started. "I'm sorry I was late coming downstairs. I had an awful hassle getting this dress on, and my hair wouldn't do what I wanted—"

"Hush, Hilly, you look wonderful. I'm almost afraid to touch you." He asked huskily, "Are you sure this isn't a fantasy? Are you my Hilly?"

"I am." She stood on tiptoe and lightly kissed his mouth. Around them, the perfume of Ed's flowers was heady. She lay her cheek against his chest, hugging him. "Tell me where you found this magnificent outfit?"

"Ed Tandy lent it to me. It was his father's wedding

suit. Ed sent away to some relatives to get it. He planned to wear it himself tonight, but the suit coat was too small around the waist, and the trousers were too long."

"I can understand that." She giggled. "I can't see Ed in this suit. But you, you're perfect."

"I heard that!" They turned and saw Ed, grinning, coming out the back door onto the deck, wearing an ordinary business suit, and Aunt Fay was ahead of him with her walker. Aunt Fay only had to use the walker another three weeks, the doctor said; then she could get around without aid, on her own two new hips.

"Hi!" Hillary called to them.

Her great-aunt whipped a lacy fan in front of her face. Her cheeks were as rosy pink as her long dress. "Hot," she said, pushing her short black hair up off her neck. "But it's better out here. Let's take an extra minute or two, Ed, then we'll go in."

"Listen, lovey"—Ed put an arm around Aunt Fay— "we'll stay out here all night if you want, in the fresh air. Shall I run these young sprouts off so we can be alone and neck a little?"

"Good grief, Tandy, act your age!"

"I am. Some might say I'm a dirty old man, but I'm not. I'm just an old man in love."

"We were about to go in and dance." Hillary laughed, catching at Nathan's warm hand. "You kids have fun!"

Chapter Fifteen

Hillary and Nathan filed back into the crowded room of dancers. She was struck with a sudden desire, a wish that her parents could be here. This was different from social affairs in Abbott. But it was that special difference that made this an event not to be missed. She couldn't think about her parents, though, and feel unhappy. Not tonight.

She spotted Lei Haffner, wearing a long, Edwardian-looking dress of cream silk. A brand-new dress she could later wear to proms, Lei had told her after she bought it. She wasn't about to wear something a person long dead had worn, she said. Funny Lei. Stratton was with her, looking pleased. Hillary smiled and waved to them, then she was in Nathan's arms, dancing close to him. It was a slow piece, that the band leader called "Love's Sweet Song." She didn't know the tune, but as far as she was concerned it couldn't have been more appropriate.

Next they swayed and swirled to a lilting piece called, "Whispering."

"Don't ever tell me again that you can't dance, Nathan Webb. You're doing a better job than I am."

"Thank my mom."

"Tell me, Nathan, please. How do you feel right now?" She had to know, hear from him, if he was happy, if he was liking this as much as she was.

"Frankly, Scarlett," he mimicked Gable, "I'm having a hell of a good time." They collided with another couple, then. Hillary saw that it was Mavina, dancing joyously with a bald, reed-thin old man, who was grinning, ear to ear.

"Ah, romance," Nathan whispered, drawing her closer.

"Isn't it wonderful?" she echoed. *Just wonderful,* she repeated silently, snuggling her face against him.

They danced to a dozen different tunes, all foreign to them. But after watching some of the oldsters for a moment or two, they accomplished a reasonable facsimile of the right steps. And Nathan's mother had done her job well. Nathan was easy to follow.

"You know, this is fun!" he exclaimed once, laughing. "I really worried about it, while I was out moving pipe. I was tempted to hide out for a few days in the cornfields, rather than come to this dance."

At intermission, they went outside and joined a group of people their age on the front lawn. Streetlights shed just enough soft glow.

"Hillary, over here!" Leilani Haffner called. "And anytime you want to come up with another good idea like this one, go ahead, Hilly."

"Then you're having a good time?"

"This ball is a blast. Isn't Stratton cute? I'm getting a

terrible crush on him, and I think it's mutual. But I might let you dance one dance with him."

"Where is Stratt?" Hillary asked.

"Inside at the refreshment table. He misses his mother's cooking, and he's trying to make up for three months away from home in one night."

Stratton Smith returned carrying a food-laden plate. He passed a tiny cupcake to Lei. "Here's what you asked for, made from all natural products, straw and carrots, I think," he joked. "Can I get you two something?" he asked Hillary.

"We were about to go inside for some punch. Have you two met? Nathan, this is Stratt Smith. Now"—she smiled up at Nathan—"want to get something to eat? The women of this town have a smorgasbord in there like you wouldn't believe."

"I don't feel hungry. I feel in love."

Lei squealed, "Oh-h-h, I knew it. I could tell by just watching you two dance. The way you look at one another, *oooh*. This is super!"

Hillary smiled at Lei, but she wished she didn't sound so junior highish. Never mind that her own heart was beating double-time tonight. "Let's go in, Nathan. I should check with Aunt Fay, too, and see if she needs anything."

"Ed's taking care of Fay, you can bet on it. But you and I can get back to dancing."

Hillary spent the remainder of the evening swaying in Nathan's arms to songs so quaint she doubted if her mother had heard of some of them. But the music soothed. Around them she saw faces of dancers looking less harried, peaceful. In that way, the ball had cast its magic, had lifted people's cares, and taken them back to the more tranquil period. As she and Aunt Fay had hoped it would.

Abby Ross should have come, it would have done her a world of good. She should have tried harder to talk her into it. Another thing, she needed to talk to Abby soon about the possibility of those houses being torn down, if she didn't know already. She meant to assure her that something was in the works, a plan to take care of the people.

Hillary thought as she was dancing that for herself, she'd never, ever felt so blissfully content and happy. She had heard a few complaints about the ball: the music was too slow for some of the livelier kids; some of the older people griped that their outfits were too warm and heavy and that their ancestors had been insane to wear them.

Nothing daunted her own joy. The evening could only go down in her book as memorable, idyllic. Maybe, she thought, giving Nathan a quick kiss, it was this guy who made it so.

After midnight, she stood with him at the foot of the stairs in the lobby, the other dancers gone. She hated saying goodnight to him. Aunt Fay had long since departed to her quarters. "I'm hungry," she said suddenly, "c'mon, let's raid the kitchen."

"Now? It must be one o'clock in the morning."

"Now."

In the kitchen, they came upon Mavina wiping off the counter as her date wolfed down a sandwich. "Wouldn't you know these starving orphans would show up?" Mavina heaved a sigh. "All right. Sit down, and I'll fix you something to eat."

"We can get something for ourselves, Mavina.

Nathan and I aren't helpless. Go on, Mavina, we can manage."

"You've convinced me. There are some leftover ribs that I roasted on the spit today. They're in the fridge, and there's potato salad. Homemade rolls and butter. Cherry tomatoes fresh from the garden in the vegetable drawer. Help yourselves, but don't you young ones stay up much longer. Good night."

When they had gone, Hillary said, "And now for some magic at the witching hour." She retrieved a pair of candles and glass holders from the pantry and placed them, lit, on the kitchen table. Nathan set out the food and found plates, while she laid the silverware and poured glasses of milk. "Isn't this romantic?" she asked before they sat down. She looked up at him, felt his arm clasp her waist. Although he said nothing, his face told her much that she wanted to know. She cleared her throat. "Sit. I'm dying of starvation."

Later, when their hunger was satisfied, and the dishes cleared, Nathan suggested that they go for a walk outside.

"Now?" she mimicked him. "It's nearly two o'clock in the a.m."

"It's tough saying goodbye to you, Hilly," he admitted, his voice both warm and serious. "I need a few more minutes with you before I take off for home. Something this difficult requires strategy. I'm not even sure I'm up to it. Why don't you just order me to leave?"

"No chance. C'mon, let's go for our walk." Outside on the deck, they stood for a moment watching the moon, high in the sky. It made the night almost as light as day. "Awesome, isn't it?" she whispered, gazing at the grounds that had looked hokey to her last spring. The difference must be that she knew now of the work and tender attention the flowers got from a dear old man she'd come to love. Beyond the yard, a shadowy moonscape with shrubs and fragrant flowerbeds, the river shone like a glittering ribbon. They left the deck and started down through the yard along the pebbled path.

In a few moments, Nathan took her gently into his arms and kissed her lightly once, twice, a third time. "Hilly, you're the most perfect girl in the world."

"You, too, Nathan. I mean you're the most wonderful person I've ever known." He did mean so very much to her. How could she live without him? It was almost September. Would she go back to Iowa and follow her plans to teach crafts to kids and study art more seriously for herself? Her heart constricted, thinking of going away from him, and she felt tears coming. She choked them back and whispered, "Oh, Nathan." What now? Now that she had found him?

WITH SUMMER NEARLY GONE, SHE WOULD HAVE TO MAKE some final decisions, Hillary was thinking as she sunned on the back deck the morning after the ball. Time had run out for wondering. She'd sized up her situation from every angle she could think of. She knew it wasn't necessary, or possible, to map out every step of the rest of her life, but she did want to plan her immediate future.

Earlier, she had thought about going back to Iowa, on her own, of course. But if she stayed in Oregon, that would put distance between herself and Mom and Dad, and in time distance might cure the hurt. No, she realized, lying with her eyes closed in the hot sun, the pain would never go away. No matter what she did or where she went, she'd never grow used to the idea that her parents wanted no more to do with her. Not when for so long each of them had shown every bit of love and care any biological parent could show a child. Where, and when, and why had things messed up? At least, returning to Iowa might provide some answers. She could build a life there. Finish school. Go to college and find out if art was what she really wanted.

But, there was Nathan. It would hurt horribly to leave him. They loved one another, but they needed time to know if their love was real, the lasting kind. What if they parted for good, only to realize years from now that this was the only true love for either of them? Too awful to consider and yet...

She grew drowsy and was almost asleep when she thought she heard Ed Tandy's voice, shouting, "Help!" She lay there, smiling to herself sleepily, wondering what mischief the old codger might be into. She needed to sort things out, to think clearly, and now that he'd awakened her, she wished he'd hush.

When Ed yelled a third time, something in his voice told Hillary that this was *real.* Her throat dried.

Something awful was happening! She jerked upright to look for Ed. He was loping, his arms waving frantically, toward the river, his abandoned hose sending a fountain of spray into the air.

She left the deck, bare feet flying, to race after him. Someone must have fallen into the river. It couldn't be Keegan and Kirstie, Nathan had told them—! At a sound behind her, she turned to see Aunt Fay in her walker, stumbling around the corner, coming down the drive in a half-run. "Who is it?" her great-aunt yelped. "What's happened?"

Hillary shook her head that she didn't know and waved her hands, sprinting hard after Ed. If this was a trick of some kind, she'd kill him, she thought. But deep down, she knew with a feeling of tightness and dread that this wasn't a joke. Someone was in trouble.

Almost to the riverbank, she shouted, "Ed, what's wrong?"

He gestured wildly down below him and fought for breath. "Sh-she walked right by me like she w-was in a trance. Her clothes on. She's trying to do away with herself! We have to help her—"

At his words, Hillary went cold all over. She reached his side and looked where he pointed. "No! Abby, no," she gasped. In the water, a few feet out from shore, Abby, her face still and deathlike, was fighting to unhook her shirt from where it had caught on a tree root. Nathan's alder. The root was all that was keeping Abby from being swept away in the current.

Without further thought, feeling desperate to reach Abby in time, Hillary plunged down the bank and leaped in close to her. In that same fleeting second, she saw Abby frantically trying to unbutton her shirt to be free of it. Cold water rushed up over Hillary's head, she fought upward with cool desperation and came up sputtering, blinking her eyes. She swished her hair back so that she could see. Quickly, she caught Abby's shoulder in a tight hold. "Please don't fight me, Abby. You don't want to die. We both will, if you give me any trouble. Please don't. I'm going to help you."

Abby's body was board stiff in her grasp. Hillary sensed the woman's tortured soul under her touch, she felt her need. "I care, Abby. I care what happens to you. You don't want to do this." Why hadn't she been a better friend to Abby, instead of always trying to avoid her? She might have seen this coming. If she'd just known how deep, how serious Abby's depression was, this might not have happened. In all the Reesville people she'd come to care about, she had *made* Abby the exception.

"Abby," she pleaded on a sob, "you have to live so I can get to know you better. I'll help, Abby. Whatever it is you want, whatever is bothering you this much, I know I can help. Give me a chance. Let's hang on to life, Abby, let's hang on." She was crying hard now, she couldn't stop herself.

A forever-seeming time passed, then Abby collapsed against her, moaning horribly. A flooding sense of relief made Hillary go weak, yet she knew she had to stay strong if she was still to get them out of this.

"My house," Abby whimpered, "they're going to take my house. Miles had no business to die. No Miles, no house—nothing."

"Abby," Hillary said firmly, "you're going to have a nice home. Nathan is seeing to it, and I'm helping him. We're going to take care of you and the others. You can't give up."

She treaded water, hanging on to Abby for dear life, praying for strength to get them to shore. Stealthily, she unhooked the back of Abby's shirt from the protruding alder root. The woman was in shock now, too far gone to notice. Then Hillary put her arm around Abby's neck, and swimming with one arm, flailing her legs, she maneuvered them to the edge, to the earthy bank. There, Ed was waiting, and he reached out and caught Abby's arm. Aunt Fay was down on her stomach, her walker discarded, and she grabbed Abby's other arm. They pulled her shoulders out of the water onto the grassy bank.

"Careful you two," Hillary gasped. "I don't want you in here." She pushed Abby's legs until the woman was all the way out of the water. Then she clambered out herself. She shoved her wet hair back from her face, wiped at the hot tears coursing down her cheeks, and knelt beside Abby.

Abby was stirring, moaning, "They're taking my house—can't go on…"

"Yes, you can," Hillary said firmly. "You're all right now, Abby. Everything is going to be fine now."

"What on earth is Abby talking about? Why did she do this?" Aunt Fay asked. Her voice was ragged with concern. "Why? Why? I had no idea she was this upset. I've had so much on my mind. The inn, my surgery—"

"We all did," Hillary agreed, smoothing Abby's wet hair back from her face.

Ed put his arms around Fay. "Now, lovey, this isn't your fault. Even if we'd known for sure the extent of Abby's depression, we still might not have been able to change a thing. Nobody can be sure. Let's just be glad we could stop her now, in time."

Mavina must have seen the commotion from a window, or heard them. She was running down the yard with Howard and another man, bringing help. Hillary sat cross-legged beside Abby, unable to leave her. She trembled, feeling immensely glad the worst was over, but knowing something had to be done for Abby. She was truly sick.

~

IN A KIND OF AFTERSHOCK, HILLARY STOOD WITH AUNT Fay and Ed, and they watched three of Aunt Fay's women friends, and the men who came with Mavina, take care of Abby. They wrapped her in a blanket and gently laid her in the back of a station wagon. After the car pulled away, with Abby lying still and pale in the back, a kind of despair hung in the air. Hillary could see that Ed and Aunt Fay looked even more drained and worn down than she was feeling. Then, a sudden rage filled Aunt Fay's face. "How come Reesville doesn't have a doctor? Why don't we have medical facilities right here, when we need them so bad, time and time again?"

Ed spoke patiently, "Fay, honey. Fay, listen to me. In that respect, the town's growth is going to have a positive effect, don't you see? When the electronics plant is in operation and the permanent population filled out, some fine doctors will see this town as a good place, financially advantageous, for them to practice medicine. A clinic or hospital can be built, in time."

Ed, too, had seen that Burton-Sipes coming was not all drawbacks. Even so, Hillary, her churlish insides still reminding her of what they'd just been through, needed to lash out at something as badly as Aunt Fay did. "They aren't doing things right, though. Burton-Sipes, I mean. When big business moves in and starts to build, it hurts people. They ought to think of people, before a stroke of anything else is done!"

It was a moment before she could go on and explain, "What finally upset Abby so badly was that she believed she wouldn't have a home anymore. Abby lives in one of those old rental houses that are set to be torn down to make way for Burton-Sipes' executives' condos. It's still undecided what will become of those people who live there now, in those houses." Hillary wiped her eyes and struggled to keep her voice. "To Abby, it was the last straw. She's responsible for her mother, her two little kids. She didn't know that Nathan is trying to make them build new homes, because I still hadn't told her, even though I meant to—"

Ed kissed Hillary's forehead tenderly, but his voice by contrast was stern. "It doesn't do one iota of good to keep piling blame on ourselves. You and Fay can quit it, or I'm going to give some hard spankings to you both. A person can't change what happened yesterday. We can only do something about now, and tomorrow."

"Ed," Hillary announced, "you're a sweetie and I love you." She hugged him. "Now, why don't you and Aunt Fay come inside? You'd both better lie down for a while; this has been rough on everybody. I'm going to get out of this wet bikini and into some jeans. Then I'm going to find Abby's house and tell her mother and the little kids what has happened."

Aunt Fay looked relieved. "I was just thinking I needed to do that, but to be honest, I don't think I can stand up any longer. Somebody should talk to the Rosses right away, and I think you'll do it best, Hilly. Let them know the truth in a way that won't worry them too much. It's probably lucky for them that Abby will be in the hands of professionals now, who can help her." She caught Ed's hand. "This old fool is right about the medical clinic too, I have to admit. Looks like we get some good with the bad, and bad with the good. I'd say that's life. Life is just bigger than all of us and keeps on rolling on its own way."

HILLARY FELT BETTER, RETURNING FROM THE ROSSES' house. As small as they were, Keegan and Kirstie seemed to understand their mother's illness. On their own, they decided they would make their mother some sugar cookies and other small gifts. Hillary promised to deliver them and to take the children to see their mother as soon as visits were allowed. The grandmother was relieved that others were in on Abby's problem, saying she'd done everything she could to try to snap Abby out of her dark mood, without success.

The house the little family was in was as decrepit as any Hillary had ever seen. Tearing it down would be no loss. The Rosses deserved better. Living in those poor conditions must have added to Abby's depression. Hillary slowed, nearing home, suddenly tired all over. Somehow, she thought, she and Nathan had to talk the county, the Burton-Sipes bosses, somebody, into providing this new housing. And if she went back to Iowa, she had to know before she left that the problem had been taken care of.

To return to Iowa, or not—she had to resolve that question, soon. Wherever she elected to go next, and whatever she did, it would be her own choosing. She felt more ready for that now.

At the inn, she crawled onto her bed, intending to lie quietly and with an open mind, make her plans. But thoughts of Abby interrupted. She'd definitely made a mistake with Abby. All the while she'd been congratulating herself on developing a new and valid interest in other people, she had intentionally let Abby slip through. She hoped she'd never make such a mistake again. She knew she would never forget that terrible struggle in the water, with life and death in the balance.

Hillary heaved a sigh. Overall, she was thankful she'd been able to pull Abby out in time. She was very glad about that. Feeling relieved, she drifted off into an exhausted sleep.

A SOFT KNOCK AT HER DOOR WOKE HER THAT EVENING. Yawning, Hillary opened the door and groggily walked into Nathan's arms. He held her tight, speaking against her hair. "Mavina peeked in for me and saw that you were asleep. I've been downstairs, waiting, ever since I heard what happened. I couldn't wait any longer to know for myself if you're okay?"

"I'm fine," she murmured lazily, pressing her face against him, feeling the warmth of his skin through his tee shirt. She drew strength, love, into herself. "Nathan, Abby Ross tried to commit suicide. I pulled her from the river just in time. But I feel so rotten that I didn't pay more attention to her, before."

"There's no guarantee it would have changed anything if you had."

"Maybe. But I'm still sorry that I ignored her. We have to do something for her, Nathan. Find a home for her and her family. Have you heard anything?"

He squeezed her tighter, and there was an undeniable thrill in his voice as he told her. "Dad wrote to the board of directors of the Burton-Sipes Corporation. Mostly to shut me up. He was sure they would ignore him. But—they answered in a very positive way that they are willing to discuss the alternate housing plan for the people on Whitman and Booth Streets."

"Congratulations, Nathan! But do you really think they'll follow through?"

"I feel positive they will. And Dad's more sure, too. It's not impossible. It wouldn't be the first time a rich company created new housing for people they are displacing, or paid for new streets, or established a bus line or something. All in the spirit of good will. I'm not saying it happens often, but it does happen."

"I'm glad you got through to all of them with your idea, Nathan. People should thank you."

"Nah." He moved his lips toward hers. "You can do it for them."

Leave Nathan? How could she, ever?

Chapter Sixteen

Hillary was glad Nathan stayed with her through dinner, holding her hand beside her plate as they ate. They were dipping into dessert, a marvelous fresh peach flambé, when Aunt Fay joined them, looking considerably refreshed. Hillary put down her spoon and laughed self-consciously when she could no longer bear the look Aunt Fay was directing her way. "Please stop looking at me as if I'm Wonder Woman."

"I can look at you however I want, young lady. And like it or not, you did a wonderful, brave thing today. I'm so proud to be your great-auntie, I could pop."

"I still feel guilty that I wasn't a better friend to Abby. She might never have tried such an awful thing."

"Well, she did, unfortunately. But you spread your wings and flew down into that river to save her. Ed and I couldn't have helped her by ourselves. Ed's heart might have given out, and I'm not back to normal yet with these hips. I got to thinking about it, after I woke up from my nap. I got on the phone and called your mother. She was so proud. She kept saying how brave her daughter is—"

Former daughter, Hillary corrected in her mind. Only words on paper. But she knew Mom well enough to know that her saving Abby's life would please her. It would have even if she'd just been a former neighbor or a casual acquaintance. "Thanks for calling the folks," she said through a tightened throat. "I was thinking of calling them, myself, later."

"You wouldn't find them at home. They've left by now, on their way here."

Hillary was stunned, and in spite of all her doubts, she felt a stab of elation. "On their way? But, why? Why would they come all the way out here to Oregon, when I may be going back to Iowa, any day?" She felt Nathan grip her hand in surprise. She was sorry, this wasn't how she wanted to give him the news.

"Can't help any of that." Aunt Fay shrugged. "They said they had to come see you, and they're taking a plane tonight. After an hour or two of sleep in Portland, they will rent a car and drive down. Likely they'll be here in Reesville before you get your sleepy head off the pillow in the morning."

"They must have some other reason for coming, not just to see me. Not because of what I did this afternoon. I don't think Mom and Dad would fly out here for me."

"Why wouldn't they?" Nathan was astonished. "They're your folks."

Aunt Fay stared at her. "Are you crazy, child? Why on earth are you talking like this?"

She didn't want to break down. She didn't want to cry in front of Aunt Fay, and especially not in front of Nathan. So she swallowed, and with effort, holding her tangled emotions in check, she told them the whole story. How she'd eavesdropped in Dad's store and learned that her father wanted to retire and take it easier. Just him and Mom, with her out of the picture. Which was justified, she added, since Mom and Dad had done so much for her for so long, and she not even their natural child, but adopted. They deserved the break, a time for themselves, now that they were getting older. And as they had wanted, she had learned this summer that she could take care of herself. That was settled.

When she was finished, Aunt Fay sat back in her chair, both arms dangling at the sides, a stupefied expression on her face. "I don't know where you got a harebrained idea like that, Hilly, but you couldn't be more wrong!"

Nathan shook his head. "You must be mistaken about this, Hilly. Your parents wouldn't dump you, not you."

She was adamant. "I know what I'm talking about. I *heard* them."

"You don't know what you're talking about," Aunt Fay said firmly. "You've actually carried this foolish, mixed-up notion in your little head the entire summer? No wonder you behaved so weirdly at times, especially whenever I mentioned your folks. Now, Hilly, honey, you've got this wrong, dead wrong, I'm telling you. But I'm going to wait and let your parents straighten you out in the morning. I can see by your face that you doubt me. But when you hear what they have to say, then you'll know. You'll believe your mother and father."

She wasn't mistaken, Hillary knew. But she gave up trying to convince Nathan and Aunt Fay. In a while, he left to go home, and Aunt Fay went to do some exercises in her room. She walked the grounds of Rainsong Inn, her mind filling of its own accord with thoughts of her parents, the way things were when she was growing up. Dad, ice skating with her at the mall rink, her mother's bedtime stories to her, so many things, so many good things.

And it seemed almost too good to be true that she would see the two of them tomorrow. Tomorrow, just a few hours away. There was no denying her feelings. She loved them, no matter what.

Hillary's eyes flew open at the first buzz of her alarm clock the next morning. As she bathed, dressed, made up her face, and brushed her hair, her hands trembled, and her stomach fluttered.

So, Mom and Dad were coming today. Here. This morning. She had considered before sleep last night that she may have gotten the wrong impression about what they wanted of her. But she could see no way she could be wrong. Today, any minute now, she would hear the answer, the truth.

They arrived before she had finished her eggs in the dining room. At the sound of their voices coming from the front of the inn, she hurried to the lobby, and there they were, hugging and exclaiming over Aunt Fay. Dad was as handsome as ever in cream slacks and a yellow shirt. Mom looked almost flowerlike in a soft floral-print dress and beige silk heels. Hillary felt choked with feeling, it was so good to see them. She fought a powerful urge to fling herself at them, but she was unsure how they would take it. She started forward slowly. "Hi, Mom. Dad. You two have a good trip?"

"Chick!" her mother cried, her eyes welling with tears although she smiled. "Come give your mora a hug. I've nearly died from missing you, honey."

She ran to them, then. Dad threw his arms wide, hugging her and Mom at the same time. Unintelligible grumbles of affection rumbled from his throat as he nuzzled her fondly. "Daddy." She kissed him, then her mother.

"We have to talk," her father said in a moment, the first of the three of them to regain his composure. "I want to hear from you, Hilly, honey, about this daring rescue you made yesterday. I want to hear about the girl, Abby Ross. We'd like to be of assistance, if she needs financial aid for medical care, or anything else."

"You bet we have to talk!" Hillary admonished, leading the way back to the dining room. They all sat down, and Mavina brought blueberry coffee cake, juice, and coffee. Aunt Fay told most of the story about Abby. How her desperation over her husband's death built up, worse than anyone realized. Until it was more than Abby could handle. And then, believing she would lose her home, too, she had wanted to end her life. Hillary brushed off their praise about the rescue.

"Now, we have some news for you, Hilly, sweetheart," her mother began. Mom looked scarcely able to still her tongue but she motioned for Dad to do the talking. "Lawrence, you tell her."

Hillary's breathing shifted into hold. She tingled all over, waiting for the official word that she was her own person now. Here it was. She'd be on her own, alone, to make her own way. So okay. Her chin lifted.

"One question first." Lawrence Germaine held his hand in the air. "Hillary, I want to know, what do you think of Oregon? Did you have a good time this summer?"

What was he getting at? Did he mean he wanted her

to stay on out here, on her own? Or was he about to grade her on her summer test of learning to be independent? Which, exactly? She believed she had passed with a fair grade. And had even learned a bit more independence than Dad had maybe bargained for. Because if they were through with her, from now on she'd make her decisions solely on her own. She was not the same young girl they'd shuttled off to Oregon last spring.

For a time, she studied her father's face. She saw, beyond his surface good looks and meticulous grooming, a boyish eagerness, an anxious expression of wanting to please. It threw her off guard. "I've—had a wonderful time, Dad," she answered hesitantly but being honest. "I've met a lot of nice people. I remember that I fought against coming here, but yes, I love Oregon. It's a great place."

"Good!" he exclaimed, clapping a palm on the table. His face was suffused with relief and happiness.

"Now, Hillary"—he sighed—"now I can tell you my plan." He looked at his wife as if to say, "I knew that I was handling this the right way."

But Aunt Fay was shaking her head in rebuttal to that look, and Hillary itched with impatience for Dad to get to the point.

"For more than a year now," he announced, "I've wanted to retire here in Oregon."

"What!" Hillary exploded, on her feet. "What?" But she saw that Dad wasn't about to allow an interruption to his happy announcement. She tightened her lips, her mind buzzing with questions.

"Judith and I are tired of the hard winters and steamy hot summers in the Midwest. We wanted to come out here to live, where we can go fishing and camping.

Where there are so many different, enjoyable opportunities for recreation. But—" His eyes found Hillary's in a soft expression. "We didn't want to move unless *you* would be happy here, too. This summer was a way to find out. We decided if you liked Oregon enough to make the move, we'd do it. We've been settling some affairs in Iowa while you were out here. How about it, love? Do we pull up stakes and move to Oregon for good?"

She would have liked to crawl into a wormhole. She sank into a chair, biting her lip. For her? They were doing this *for* her, and not—she stammered, blinking away tears, "M-move here to Oregon? But I was sure—I thought you didn't want—" Aunt Fay frantically signaled her to shut her mouth. Of course! Of course she couldn't tell them that she had thought they were *finished with her.* How could she have thought such a thing? What was such a strong conviction earlier crumbled now in a wake of pain. Mom and Dad would be so hurt if they knew her faith in them, and in their love, was that shallow. She'd just been childish, dumb.

And if she hadn't been so concerned about *herself,* her summer, what she wanted to do, she might not have been so quick to jump to such a crazy conclusion. What about Dad, though? He could have done things differently, too. She stared at him. He had no right to treat her like a silly, ignorant little girl who wouldn't care. Who wouldn't understand her parents' wishes, their problems. Keeping a secret like that, deceiving her, really.

But, back then, would she have understood? Last May, if Dad had told her the truth straight out, what would she have done? Knowing, she flushed, and lifted her water glass up in front of her face, gazing into it as if it were a crystal ball. She'd have rebelled. She'd have fought a permanent move to Oregon like crazy. And most likely her parents would have given in to her. They would have given up their own dream.

Her mother's voice broke into her thoughts. "You won't mind doing your last year of high school here?"

Hillary set the glass down thoughtfully. She smiled and shook her head, "Not at all. The plans I've made would work out here." After school and on weekends she could go on working at the inn, that would take care of having a part-time job. She liked the feeling of self-reliance that gave. She'd continue to explore the field of art. And if she could make the time, there were changes coming to this town that she'd like to get involved in. She could volunteer her services, or even create a job she might be paid to do. And in the older section of Reesville, those Victorian homes that were solid enough should be preserved. Maybe she could be the one to initiate that historic preservation group to protect them. There was so much here she'd love to be part of. Still another thought struck her, why, Nathan, she could—!

"And you'll choose an Oregon college next year and live at home with us?" It was Pop this time who brought her back to the immediate conversation. He looked at her when she didn't answer right away and amended, "Or at least you'll be close enough so your mother and I can see you on weekends and holidays?"

So Dad was catching on that she wasn't the same kid he and Mom shanghaied onto that plane in Des Moines. Good. "That's another year away, Dad," she said, rising to kiss him on the forehead. "We'll see." Truthfully, she felt like thanking Mom and Dad. Not for sending her here, not only for that. But for causing her own mistaken belief that had brought her to herself, her better self.

She'd think of a way to do it, too, without letting them know her dumb belief.

"Pop?" she said in a moment, dazzling him with a grin. "Could you and Mom excuse me? I promised to meet a friend down by the river this morning. I want you guys to meet him, so stay right here, and I'll bring him back with me."

She hurried out onto the deck. Far down by the river, Nathan sat at one of the picnic tables. He leaned back, facing the inn, waiting for her. Of all the new people she'd gotten to know this summer, he was the best.

She didn't regret the other guys, having all those dates. Gorgeous guys, plain guys, and guys in between. Knowing different guys gave a girl a basis for comparison. That was important, she thought, if and when a girl decided to get married.

Again she was reminded that her world back in Iowa had been pretty narrow and indulged. She was beginning to see that this big, wide wonderful world was truly many kinds of worlds. This summer she'd sampled one of them, and in the future she wanted to sample many, many more. Explore, learn, grow. And whatever the future might have in store, she knew she would never forget this Oregon summer. Or the tall, dark-haired boy getting to his feet, grinning, ambling toward her. Maybe, just maybe, he had a place in that future. Only time would tell. Not just another gorgeous guy, Nathan was a gorgeous guy and more, with wonderful goals. Best of all, he was her summer love.

She reached him, just as Ed popped up unexpectedly from behind a red rosebush. Ed winked at her, just as Nathan put his arms about her. "Now remember the rules!" the old man crowed.

"What does he mean? What rules?" Nathan whispered.

"I don't know." Hillary laughed. "I've never known what rules Ed is talking about."

"Good. We'll make our own." And Nathan kissed her.

A look at: Willow Whip

From award-winning author Irene Bennett Brown comes a heartwarming story of a young girl determined to make it possible for her constantly moving farmer family to buy a farm that she has come to love and wants to live on permanently.

Could the Faber family really afford a farm of their own? Could they stop moving from place to place? Her father has almost given up hope, but for Willow Faber, the only dream worth having is a farm of their own.

The Fabers are tenant farmers. They move almost every year trying to find a better place. But no farm will ever compare to the one Willow calls "The Ranch." Once a Pony Express stop, it is old, but solid and pleasant, and Willow is willing to do everything she can to make it theirs.

For a long year Willow does little but plan and work and save, pushing herself—and her family—to the brink, earning herself the nickname "Willow The Whip." She sacrifices everything, including all of the things she had hoped to gain by staying in one place. Only near disaster helps her understand what she has lost and all that she still has to gain.

AVAILABLE NOW

About the Author

Irene Bennett Brown is an award-winning author who enjoys using Kansas—where she was born—as background for her historical novels. Previous to her ten novels for adults, Brown authored nine young adult novels. *Before the Lark* won a Western Writers of America Spur Award, was nominated for the Mark Twain Award, and received other honors. Her other YA novels include *To Rainbow Valley, Run from a Scarecrow, Skitterbrain, Willow Whip, Morning Glory Afternoon, Answer Me Answer Me, I Loved You Logan McGee, and Just Another Gorgeous Guy.*

Her most recent Nickel Hill series include *Miss Royal's Mules, Tangled Times, Somebody's Business* and *One True Deed.* All are adult sequels to *Before the Lark.*

She lives with her husband, Bob—a retired research chemist—on two fruitful acres along the Santiam River in Oregon.

Visit her website at irenebennettbrown.net for more information.